PRIMAL
ORIGIN

JACK SILKSTONE

BOOKS

By Jack Silkstone

The Primal Series

PRIMAL Origin

PRIMAL Unleashed

PRIMAL Vengeance

PRIMAL Fury

PRIMAL Reckoning

PRIMAL Nemesis

PRIMAL Redemption

PRIMAL Renegade

PRIMAL Deception

PRIMAL Exodus

PRIMAL books are dedicated to those who have fought for a just cause.

Vinci Books

vinci-books.com

Published by Vinci Books Ltd in 2025

1

Chapter One

ABU DHABI, 2004

THE US EMBASSY in Abu Dhabi didn't impress Vance. Like so many other buildings in the Emirates, it was a monstrosity of steel and glass, chilled to almost arctic temperatures by an army of air conditioners. A CIA para-military officer, the solidly built African American wasn't bothered by the heat of the Arabian Gulf. He'd been in the country for over a month and was fully acclimatized. So much so, he was shivering as he waited for an audience with the ambassador.

"They always have it up too high," the secretary said.

Vance attempted a smile. "Yeah, it keeps the penguins working."

The pretty blonde laughed and returned her attention to her computer.

He scanned the room again. It was lavishly furnished, some new vogue designer's attempt to give it some warmth. The marble floor was laid with ornamental Persian rugs.

Expensive paintings graced the walls on either side of a pair of solid mahogany doors that barred entry into the ambassador's office. It was nothing like the rough compound he'd called home for the past five weeks.

Vance and his offsider, a former Marine known as Ice, were working with a World Health Organization team in an industrial sector of the desert city. They had established a health clinic to support thousands of the city's impoverished workers. In a US Government-sponsored initiative, the team was currently checking for any signs of a superflu pandemic.

From Vance's perspective, the WHO team was providing cover for the CIA to track down a terrorist group. In the last month, a spate of suicide attacks had rocked the Gulf States, targeting Western expatriates and government officials. CIA analysts had assessed that the attacks were linked to the recent US invasion of Iraq. However, one of the suicide bombers had been identified as Bangladeshi, recruited from the UAE's immigrant workforce.

Vance and Ice had been sent to Abu Dhabi to track down the recruiters and follow the link back to the terrorist command structure. So far the few leads they'd uncovered had been dead ends. Despite this, Vance's experience and gut instinct told him they were hunting in the right place.

A buzzer sounded on the secretary's desk. "Sir, the ambassador will see you now." She rose and walked across to open the solid wooden doors.

Vance extracted his muscular frame from the sofa and followed her into the ambassador's office. The opulence of the waiting area was magnified tenfold in the huge room. Tall, blast-proof, tinted windows reduced the sun's glare but allowed a sweeping view of the malls, hotels, and high-rises that had sprouted from the oil-rich sands of Abu Dhabi.

This was the office of a man at home with wealth and power.

Howard D. Beecroft sat behind his antique desk and examined Vance with a critical eye. He noted with scorn the dusty boots, grubby khaki cargo pants, and faded blue shirt. His gaze lingered on the weathered features of the CIA veteran.

"So this is the renegade running black ops in my Emirates," Beecroft said.

"I'm sorry: black ops?" Vance returned the scornful gaze, equally unimpressed with the bureaucrat.

Beecroft sported a portly frame and ruddy complexion, the result of years on the cocktail circuit. "Yes, the CIA didn't seek my approval for your little mission." His chins wobbled as he spoke.

"Last time I checked, the CIA didn't work for the State Department."

Beecroft tipped back in his soft leather chair. His belly strained against a tailored waistcoat under a dark blue suit. Vance almost expected to see a gold chain disappearing into the vest pocket.

"I don't think you understand, Mr...." The ambassador paused, unable to recall Vance's surname. "I don't think you understand just how important the Emirates is to America. The lifeblood of our nation flows through this relationship and it is my job to ensure that nothing damages that. That no obstacles block the flow. Obstacles like you."

Vance's brow furrowed. "Don't get me wrong, I understand the situation. But what I don't get is how a discreet CIA operation could be considered an obstacle."

"Discreet? Is that what you think your little mission is?" Beecroft selected a manila folder from a pile on his desk. "If it is so discreet, then explain to me why the head of the

Special Tasks Branch is sending me reports warning that you are, in fact, the next target for the very terrorists you're supposed to be hunting?"

He threw the folder on the desk. "Your operation has the potential to severely embarrass my standing with the Emir. I can only hope that he isn't aware of your activities already."

Vance stepped forward to pick up the folder. It contained a single-page police report. He skimmed it and dropped it back on the desk. "How the hell did they find out we're here?"

"Evidently your World Health Organization cover isn't as good as you think."

"I call bullshit on that, Mr. Ambassador."

"How it happened doesn't matter." Beecroft waved his finger as he spoke. "The simple fact is you've been compromised and now you're out. I'm sure you can hunt terrorists in Iraq or Afghanistan. My aide has arranged tickets for you and the—"

"Get the WHO team out, but I'm staying."

Beecroft pushed back his chair and struggled to remove his corpulent frame from its clutches. He finally got to his feet, drawing himself up to his full five feet nine inches. "You will do no such thing. This is my post and I will—"

"You will sit the fuck down, Ambassador!" Vance growled from a height advantage of almost six inches.

Beecroft shrunk like a deflated balloon, dropping back into his chair.

"The only way we could have been compromised is through this office."

The ambassador opened his mouth to object but Vance cut him off again. "Now. You're probably not harboring Bin

4

Laden and co, so my guess is you blabbed to one of your buddies at poker."

Beecroft opened his mouth to protest, but thought better of it.

"Now usually I would get very, very upset about that, but this time I'm gonna let it slide. What I won't be doing is getting on any airplane."

The ambassador's face turned a brighter shade of red. "You will get on that plane. Otherwise I will submit a report to Washington."

Vance smiled. "You go right ahead and do that, Mr. Ambassador. By the time your report gets read and someone takes notice, my job here will be done. So you just get back to protecting the flow of oil and I'll get back to tracking down our nation's enemies." He turned and walked toward the door.

"This will be the end of you, Vance. I'll make sure of that."

"Take your best shot, Mr. Ambassador. Better men have tried."

————

ICE WAS WAITING in the parking lot when Vance exited the building. He wore similar clothes to the senior CIA operative: tan cargo pants and a loose-fitting shirt. The former recon Marine was chatting with a member of the Embassy's Marine security detail. The guard was a big man, at least six feet, but the paramilitary operative towered over him. With short blond hair, a square jaw, and the build of an NFL quarterback, Ice was a formidable-looking individual.

Spotting Vance, he shook hands with the Marine and

walked back to their Toyota Land Cruiser, starting the engine.

Neither man said a word as Ice drove them from the embassy, until the battered four-wheel drive had merged into Abu Dhabi's hectic traffic.

"Where we heading, boss?" Ice asked.

"Find a place to park. I need to make a few calls."

"That bad?"

"Yes and no." Vance gave him a rundown on the conversation with the ambassador. "If the police report is accurate, we've been compromised and now the hunter has become the hunted," he concluded.

"There's more good in this than bad," Ice said after a moment.

"How's that, big man?"

"The way I see it, the ambassador's done us a favor. Now we know for sure that this terrorist group has links to the Emirates government. We just need to flush them out."

Vance looked sideways. "Ice, you're nuts. I tell you a bunch of jihadist douche bags are gonna try and blow us to hell and you think it's a good thing." He shook his head and laughed.

The corner of Ice's mouth turned up in a slight smile. His eyes never left the packed highway.

Vance continued. "Only problem is that pompous cock-sucker has given us the boot. It won't take Langley long to follow that up and shit-can us."

"Means we need to move fast."

"Yep. First things first, we get the Doc and his crew out." Vance pulled out his phone and scrolled through the contacts, looking for the physician in charge of the WHO team. "After that I'll arrange a meeting with Tariq and find out how Special Tasks were alerted to the attack. You check if the gear has arrived."

Ice pulled into the parking lot of one of Abu Dhabi's shopping malls and slotted the four-wheel drive into a free spot. Vance was already talking to the head of the WHO team. Ice jumped out of the vehicle and dialed the FedEx Custom Critical depot to check if the extra equipment he'd ordered from Langley had arrived. With a direct threat to the team, he'd be happier packing a little extra heat.

Chapter Two

AN HOUR LATER, Vance was waiting in an emergency fire escape at the Al Wahda shopping mall. A symbol of the Gulf city's progress, the mall was a sprawling complex of over 120 high-end retail outlets. Vance hated it, all sparkling marble and glass, built by unskilled immigrant labor with petrodollars. Like so many things in the Middle East, the glamor was a thin veil. In the staircase, behind the scenes, the flaking paint and exposed wiring told another story.

Vance checked his phone. His contact was late. A moment later it buzzed and a message displayed on the screen:

Contact is moving toward your loc

Ice was watching the approaches to the emergency exit. Despite his stature, the CIA operative had an uncanny knack for remaining out of sight. Vance felt comfortable knowing the big man had his back.

The door swung open and a man in a dark suit barged

in. He gave Vance a cursory nod and scanned the stairwell. Vance lifted his arms, allowing himself to be patted down. Security procedures complete, the man exited through the same door. A few seconds later Vance's contact entered.

"It is good to see you again, Vance." Tariq Ahmed, the head of Abu Dhabi's Police Special Tasks Branch, was every inch the charming gentleman, his slim frame clad in an immaculately tailored suit, dark hair slicked back, beard and mustache trimmed to perfection.

"You too, Tariq. Been a while."

Prior to assuming his current mantle, Tariq had been an intelligence officer in the UAE Army. He had worked with Vance in Afghanistan.

Tariq's face remained impassive as he spoke. "I wish we were meeting under better circumstances." He folded his arms across his chest. "You should have listened to Mr. Beecroft."

"What the hell, Tariq? Goddamn tangos want to take down my team and you're going to let a pen pusher like Beecroft stop me from taking them out?"

"Mr. Beecroft is a powerful man. If you value your career, I would suggest you follow his direction."

"My career? Tariq, I've been in this business for long enough and one thing I've learned is that Langley doesn't give a shit about me. No, this is personal now. I want these jihadi fucks head's on a slab!"

Tariq raised an eyebrow at the tirade. "As do I, Vance, and I assure you we have the situation well in hand."

"Yeah, twelve dead in three months. Looks like you've got it well in hand." Vance gave a hard stare. "Does it bother you that someone in your government is sponsoring the murder of innocent civilians?"

Tariq's eyes narrowed. "How do you know that?"

"I didn't, but I suspected as much. Now you've all but confirmed it."

"There is more to this than you think, my friend."

"Clearly. That's why you're meeting me in a goddamn stairwell."

"Leave this to my people; the CIA has no role to play here. This is an Emirates problem and we will resolve it. You should focus on Iraq."

It was Vance's turn to fold his arms. "No role? You feed us some crap about a terrorist group targeting my team and then you tell me I don't have a role to play in it. Screw you, Tariq, I thought we were friends."

"We are, and that is why you were warned."

"Don't think I'm not appreciative, buddy, but you need to give me a whole lot more than that. Who's your source?"

"I cannot reveal that."

"Then give me some details. Who's leading the attack? When's it planned for? What type of attack? A suicide bomber? A car bomb?"

"The attack was to occur in the next twenty-four hours; a VBIED into the medical clinic. That is all I know."

Vance didn't believe for one second that the well-groomed Arab was sharing everything.

"Listen, trust me when I say this." Tariq's gaze softened slightly. "There is nothing more the CIA can do here. Your embassy has booked a flight for you tonight. You would be well advised to take it."

There was silence as the two men stared at each other.

"Maybe you're right," Vance said.

Tariq smiled halfheartedly. "You're making the right decision, my friend. Have a safe trip and perhaps we will meet again under better circumstances." With that, the head of Special Tasks Branch disappeared through the door.

Vance waited a few seconds before moving down the stairs to the underground parking level. He exited the stairwell and walked across to where the Land Cruiser was parked.

A few minutes later Ice joined him. "Only the one guy with him, Vance. He's trying to keep it discreet."

"Yeah, could mean he's being watched."

"Do you trust him?"

Vance shook his head. "I'm not sure, but I'd wager he knows a shitload more than he's telling."

"Any more intel on the threat?"

"Yeah. Car bomb into the compound. Next twenty-four hours."

"Think it's reliable?"

"Tariq and I worked together in the 'Ghan. He pulled my nuts out of the fire a couple of times. If it wasn't for him, I would've ended my run holding my own head on YouTube." Vance opened his car door. "So yeah, I think it's good. I've just got the feeling he's still hiding something from us."

They climbed into the Land Cruiser and Ice started the engine. "From what I've read in *Forbes*, his father's a very powerful man."

"Damn straight he is. The emir's chief security advisor, and in his spare time he runs a multi-billion dollar logistics company."

"So if Tariq's hiding something, it's gotta be big." The tires of the four-wheel drive screeched on the polished concrete as Ice nosed it toward the exit.

"You're right. If we uncover a terrorist cell operating inside the UAE government, it would be a major embarrassment. That's why he wants the CIA out. Not that it would matter. That prick Beecroft would sacrifice his own mother to keep the oil flowing."

"The terrorists could have a royal link," added Ice.

"True. Some rich, bored asshole getting his kicks out of playing jihad. Whoever it is, he fucked up though."

"How so?"

"By trying to kill us."

"So what's the plan from here?" Ice asked as he lowered the window and paid the foreign worker who manned the parking booth.

"We get our gear from the depot and stake out the clinic. Jihad jerk-off's posse are bound to do one last recon. We'll leave the lights on and maybe they'll still be keen to join our little party."

Chapter Three

DESPITE BEING the home of over five thousand immigrant workers, Abu Dhabi's Musaffah industrial complex was deathly quiet under the dark shroud of a moonless night. Vance had parked the Land Cruiser in a side alley around the corner from the WHO clinic, hidden from view but still positioned to allow quick access to the street. On the seat next to him was a laptop, the screen displaying images beamed from two cameras hidden on the high walls of the WHO compound. One showed a view down the street to the front, the other covered the narrow alley that ran behind.

Vance panned a camera to the construction site opposite the clinic. The street lighting was dim and the green hue of the infrared camera made the half-built sheds look like the skeleton of a prehistoric beast. A cat, hunting rats in the rubble of the building site, leaped from a Dumpster, landing gracefully alongside a pile of builder's waste.

"Here, kitty, kitty," Ice's voice came through over the radio.

Vance watched the cat arch its back and streak away into the darkness. He panned the camera back over the area. "Damn, Ice, I can't see you. I'm looking straight at that heap of crap you're under."

"I'm a trash ninja," quipped Ice. His tone changed. "Vehicle approaching."

A battered pickup approached down the street, its head-lights off.

Ice gripped his silenced Beretta tightly and flicked the safety off. "This looks suspect."

Vance panned the camera toward the threat.

The pickup coasted down the street, slowing in front of the clinic, and came to a halt directly opposite Ice. It paused, then veered toward him, bouncing over the low curb.

"Shit," whispered Vance as it stopped mere feet from his hidden partner. The doors opened and two men wearing dark clothes jumped down from the cab.

Ice slid one hand under his body, ready to spring from his hiding spot.

"These guys look like some sort of amateur recon team," whispered Vance as he watched them through the camera.

Ice clicked his transmit button once in response. One of the men was standing almost directly on top of him. The one closest to Ice moved around the vehicle into the shadows cast by the lights of the compound. The truck now separated them from Ice.

The two men just stood in the shadows watching the street. Minutes passed before Ice whispered, "What's the plan? Take one down and get the other to talk?"

"Negative. Something's not right, just sit tight."

A moment later the two men began moving around the

construction site. They talked in hushed voices and used a flashlight to probe the piles of building materials.

"I think we've got ourselves some lowbrow thieves," whispered Ice.

"Roger."

The scavengers attempted to load a heavy metal beam into the back of their pickup. A set of headlights flashed down the road and they dropped it with a crash. Vance smirked as the would-be thieves clambered to find a hiding spot behind their truck. He focused the camera on the approaching vehicle. It was a Mercedes, not unusual for Abu Dhabi.

"You got eyes on?" he asked over the radio.

"Yes," Ice whispered.

The saloon slowed almost to a halt as it passed by. On his screen Vance could make out a faint glow on the passenger-side window. It took him a second to realize what it was; a video camera.

"These are our guys, Ice. Tag 'em."

As the Mercedes accelerated from the clinic, Ice broke cover. The pile of trash materialized into a man wielding a gun. The two would-be thieves, startled, ran yelling into the building site, tripping over the debris.

Ice aimed the Tippmann paintball marker at the Mercedes and squeezed the trigger. The ball left the barrel with a snort and slapped the rear right wheel. It burst, spraying a clear liquid across the side of the car.

"That's a hit," reported Ice.

"Nice shot. Now let's find out where these clowns are hanging out."

Chapter Four

SIX HUNDRED MILES above Abu Dhabi, a satellite adjusted its sensor array on an isolated bandwidth of radiation. Within a few seconds it had located a target. A complex algorithm converted the information into a military grid reference and relayed it to the requesting entity.

Back on the ground, Ice had joined Vance in the Land Cruiser. He was still wearing his combat rig, a balaclava rolled up on top of his head.

"You smell like shit!" Vance said as he hunched over his laptop.

"Next time I'll sit in the car while you crawl in the trash."

"No thanks, bud. I'm getting too old for all that sneaky peeky crap."

"Have we got a track?"

"I've got the grid. Plotting it now." Vance opened the mapping program and entered the grid reference from the satellite. "Target's about four miles away, still in the industrial sector. Looks like a medium-size warehouse with a high brick wall." Vance handed the laptop to Ice and started the car. "You're the shooter, Ice. How we gonna crack this one?"

Ice had planned hundreds of raids in Afghanistan and Iraq. "I think we're going to have to get in close."

It took a little over ten minutes to cover the distance to the warehouse. They parked a few hundred yards out and advanced on foot. Both men were equipped similarly: combat body armor worn over their shirts and Nomex bala-clavas covering their faces. They carried suppressed weapons; the last thing they wanted was to alert the local authorities. Ice favored a UMP45 submachine gun and Vance a M4 CQBR carbine.

They hugged the shadows as they moved stealthily to the twelve-foot brick wall surrounding the target warehouse. The only entry point was a well-lit steel sliding gate.

Crouched in a ditch beside the wall, Ice pulled a compact screen from his vest. He uncoiled a flexible camera and plugged it into the device. With Vance scanning for threats, he stood and held the setup at arm's length, allowing the camera to see over the wall. He panned it back and forth, recording imagery.

Seconds later he was back in the ditch reviewing the footage with Vance. "There's the Mercedes. No sign of anyone; they might be all in bed."

"I doubt it. They're probably going over their recon footage."

"We should drop in for a critique."

"Any wire on that wall?" Vance peered closer at the screen.

"Negative. Your balls are safe."

Ice packed the camera away and followed Vance over the wall. He slid across the top of the brickwork and dropped onto the gravel parking lot in front of the warehouse. The Mercedes was parked in front of a roller door. A smaller entrance was off to the right and Ice guessed it led into the building's office.

They followed the wall around, avoiding the light from above the front gate. As they neared the entrance, Ice signaled to halt. He left Vance in cover and crawled to the office door. The tiny camera snaked under the rubber seal at the bottom, giving an insect's view inside.

It was unoccupied with a single light illuminating a desk and chairs. An AK assault rifle was on the desk; Ice could make out the distinctive stock, along with a pair of night-vision goggles and a laptop. He relayed his findings to Vance over the radio.

"It's your call, big man."

"Silent entry. I'll lead." Ice turned the door handle. It wasn't locked. With a click, the door popped inward. He pushed it open and crept inside.

He froze. At the other side of the room, standing in the next doorway was a young man in white robes. They stared at each other for a moment, until the youth dove for the AK on the table. Ice's UMP spat twice and the heavy slugs tore into the target's torso. The body smashed into the table with a crash.

"Shit," whispered Vance as he stepped into the office.

Ice was already moving. He stepped around the body and through the next door. Bright overhead lighting caused him to squint as he entered the open space of the warehouse. He sensed a tall figure lurch at him from the side. A blow knocked the UMP from his hands and it dropped onto its sling. He reacted by swinging his right arm in an arc, pushing his assailant's pistol up against the wall.

He turned his face away as a blow impacted on the side of his head. His vision flashed red and he staggered. With his right arm pinning the pistol to the wall, he spun his left elbow, driving it into the face of the attacker. There was a crunch and a crash as a man fell backward against the sheet-metal wall. Before the body hit the floor, Ice swung his UMP up, and fired a burst into its chest.

In the few seconds it had taken Ice to dispatch his assailant, Vance had calmly stepped past. Deeper into the warehouse another man in white raised a pistol. Vance shot him twice in the face, his suppressed carbine making a sharp, slapping noise. The 5.56mm bullets punched through soft bone and tissue. The man dropped like a puppet with its strings cut.

The warehouse was new, shelves on the walls still empty. A white minivan was parked facing him. Vance noted it was sitting low on its axles. The smell of fuel hung in the air.

Faintly, above the hum of the fluorescent lighting, Vance could hear chanting. It was coming from the van. He padded cautiously toward the vehicle, his weapon tight against his shoulder. As he approached the rear with a series of shuffling side steps, the red dot of his Aimpoint sight came to rest on the forehead of another young man. This one was sitting in the back of the van, eyes wide, chanting softly to himself.

"Ice, we've got a big fucking problem."

"Moving."

In the back of the van, the teenager was sitting on a layer of small bricks wrapped in wax paper. He was clutching what looked like a slot-car controller.

"Release-activated detonator," Ice stated from behind Vance, "and probably at least half a ton of C4."

"I've seen this before," said Vance. "You see how he's clean-shaven, head and all. I've seen this before in Yemen. He's been purified for the big bang. Poor bastard's well and truly been brainwashed."

"None of them are Arabs, except maybe the big one by the door. At a guess I'd say this guy's Pakistani."

Vance lowered his carbine and pulled off his balaclava. "It's OK, son. You don't need to do this. Just hand me the clacker, alright?" He reached out with one hand.

The boy's eyes grew even wider and his chanting more earnest. He threw his hands in the air with a scream, "*ALLAHU AKBA—*"

There was a thud as Ice shot him cleanly through the head. The body fell backward, blood splashing across the bricks of C4.

Both of them waited for the flash that would send them to the afterlife.

"How the fuck are we still alive?" Vance asked in a low voice.

Ice climbed into the van and picked up the remote from where it had fallen. He traced the cable, lifting blocks of explosives to reveal the detonation system. The wire ran into a simple circuit with a battery and a cell phone. Electric cables like the arms of an octopus snaked out to half a dozen detonators embedded in the C4. Ice cut the circuit board free and held it up to the light. "The remote's a dummy. Whoever set this up didn't trust his bomber. The phone's the only way to activate it."

Ice tore the phone from the circuit and passed it to Vance. It began vibrating and a buzzing filled the air. Vance spun around, eyes searching the room. He sprinted across to the man who had attacked Ice earlier.

Unlike the three youths, this guy was big, at least six feet, with a heavy build. His face was dark and angular with a hawk-like nose. Ice's bullets had torn into his chest and he was lying in a growing pool of thick blood, a cell phone clutched in his hand. Vance crouched over him and held out the other buzzing phone.

"Looking for this, motherfucker?"

The man coughed. Blood ran out of his mouth and down his neck. He wasn't going to last much longer.

"Who do you work for?" Vance growled as he grabbed the Arab by his shoulders and effortlessly propped him against the wall. If he could stop the lungs from filling, maybe he could keep him alive a little longer.

"You—you should have gone home, CIA pig," coughed the man. "You're a dead man now."

"You and your buddies had your chance, pal. Now how about you tell me who you're working for and maybe I won't go after your family."

"Maybe... you should... ask your friend, Tariq." With that, the man's head slumped against his chest.

Vance checked for a pulse.

"Dead?" yelled Ice from the next room.

"Yep." Vance scrolled through the man's phone. It only had the one number saved in the contacts. He emptied the corpse's pockets and pulled out a wallet. "You're not gonna believe it, Ice. He's Emirates Police. One Yussuf Bishara."

"That makes sense. Check this out."

Vance walked into the office where Ice was standing over the desk, scrolling through a presentation on the laptop.

"Pretty damn slick," observed Vance. The slides showed

a detailed plan for the attack on the WHO clinic, complete with surveillance photos.

"Whoever put this together was a pro: definitely military, cops, or intel," agreed Ice.

Vance stared at the screen for a few seconds, then looked up. "Grab the laptop. I'll take some photos and we'll get the hell out of here. I want to have another chat with our man Tariq."

Chapter Five

BY THE TIME Vance located the head of Special Tasks Branch, the sun was peeking over the desert horizon. One of his contacts had a source in the Hotel La Capiard, a favorite breakfast spot of Tariq Ahmed. The opulent establishment was owned by none other than Tariq's father, Hussein Ahmed, CEO of Lascar Logistics and security adviser to the emir.

The wheels of the Land Cruiser screamed as Vance sped around the roundabout at the front of the hotel and screeched to a halt next to a Rolls-Royce. The owner, a sheik dressed in traditional Arabic robes, glared at the two grubby Americans as they ran up the entrance stairs.

Even without their weapons and body armor, the two big men looked menacing. Hotel security stood shocked as Vance and Ice barged into the lobby. The two Special Tasks agents guarding the door to the hotel restaurant were not as compliant.

The larger of the two recognized Vance and walked

forward, gesturing for him to stop. Vance dropped him with a punch to the face.

Seeing his partner felled with a single blow, the other man reached for his pistol. Ice grabbed the weapon as it left the holster, twisting it out of the officer's hand. He spun the man into a headlock and pressed the weapon up against his temple.

There was only one customer actually dining in the restaurant; the exclusive venue was only open to the public in the evenings. The half-dozen men on the other tables reacted quickly, drawing a variety of weapons. The two CIA officers found themselves looking down the barrels of no less than two submachine guns and four pistols.

Tariq glared at them from his table. He took a napkin from his lap and wiped the corner of his mouth. "Let them in."

His men lowered their weapons and Ice released his captive. A waiter appeared and guided them to the table.

Tariq waited for them to sit. "I thought I might be seeing you gentlemen again."

Vance threw a bloodied ID card onto the table. "We got caught up. Ran into someone you know."

Tariq glanced at the card and waved his men out of the room. "As you can see, Vance, this problem of mine is complicated."

"No shit!"

"You put me in a very precarious position. You have no idea how powerful these men are." He gestured to the ID. "They have people everywhere."

"I got a pretty good idea who the fuck they are, Tariq." He glanced at the ID card. "Our mutual buddy here's one of the emir's personal bodyguards." Vance's face was expressionless as he stared across the table.

A waiter deposited a tray of pastries and scurried away. Ice picked up a chocolate croissant and bit into it. "Vance, you really should try one of these, they're great."

Vance selected one of the pastries. "Are you sure there's nothing you want to tell us, Tariq?"

Tariq sat upright in his chair. "If we take on these men and we fail, we lose everything. If you want a part in this, you must understand that rules no longer apply."

Ice finished his croissant, wiping his hands on a napkin. They left a black smudge on the pristine white cloth. "I don't know you very well, sir, but it seems to me that the only person you would fear in the whole of the UAE would be the emir, or maybe one of his most trusted advisers."

The Arab's face hardened.

Vance stared at him in disbelief. "You're shitting me. We're right, aren't we? Your father, Hussein Ahmed, is a goddamn terrorist."

Tariq considered his words carefully. "I have always known that my father harbored animosity toward the Western world. It is only recently that I have become aware of his extra activities."

"Jesus! Your father is a billionaire with access to the ear of one of the most powerful Arabs in the world. He makes Bin Laden look like a pauper."

"Yes. Now can you understand why we must be so careful? If we are to defeat him we must—"

"Hang on a second," said Ice. "'We?' I thought 'we' weren't invited to this little party of yours."

"Not at all. I extended your organization an invitation from the beginning."

"You sneaky bastard," said Vance. "The initial tip-off on the terrorist cell. The link to the immigrant workers. That was you!"

Tariq nodded. "I needed external support."

"And the meeting in the stairwell. You knew I wasn't gonna fly home. You knew I'd go after them."

Tariq smiled. "I needed you. I am not sure how deep the infiltration into my own organization goes but many of my men are loyal to my father. He continues to surround me with his followers."

"How did you know the CIA would send me?" Vance asked.

"That, my friend, was Allah's will, or perhaps it was because I asked for you personally. It depends on what you believe."

"So what are we going to do now?" asked Ice. "Do we take this to Langley?"

"And what will they do?" Tariq asked in return. "Do you think the CIA will approve his assassination? That is the only way to stop him. You are either a fool or naive, Mr. Ice. Your masters are more than aware of my father's ties and they would not dare risk killing him. Hussein and the Emir are like brothers, and men like Howard Beecroft will not jeopardize their precious oil."

"I don't give a shit about Beecroft," said Vance, glancing at Ice.

The big man nodded.

Vance continued. "No doubt you have plans of your own, Tariq?"

There was silence at the table as Tariq made his decision. "As you know, my father is the sole owner of Lascar Logistics. The company is legitimate, worth over 1.2 billion dollars, and has nearly two hundred aircraft across the globe." Tariq waved over the waiter and ordered another coffee before continuing.

"I have recently become aware that within the structure

of my father's company is a small department called Priority Movements Airlift. What is interesting about this department is it consumes capital but doesn't create revenue." Tariq paused as the waiter brought out his coffee. "What is also interesting is that, despite having five aircraft on paper, the department actually has no physical fleet."

Vance interrupted. "It's a front."

"Correct. It is how my father channels funds into his many extremist ventures."

Tariq took a sip from his coffee. "Eventually, when I inherit my father's fortune, I intend to use this funding to finance an independent counterterrorism capability." He stretched out his hands. "Turn the tables, if you will."

"Your own private army to track down Al-Qaeda?" asked Ice.

"No. An independent organization to target evil and bring those who perpetrate it to justice, regardless of religion or politics. Men like my father cannot be allowed to bring misery to the world and go unchecked."

Vance could see where this was going. Tariq knew the CIA operatives were jaded and he was offering them a job, a unique opportunity to start a new organization, one dedicated to making a difference. There was only one obstacle. "So, no love lost between you and your father?"

The Arab's features darkened with rage. "I watched him beat my mother till she could no longer stand. Why? Because she dared to look him in the eye. When she died, my loyalty to my family died with her. My father and I share a very different view of the world and I owe him nothing."

"And now you want him dead," Vance said.

"That would be my preferred outcome."

Vance looked across at his partner. Ice nodded.

"That we can probably help you with."

WHEN VANCE and Ice returned to the terrorist warehouse it reeked of death; death mixed with the stench of high explosives. They piled the bodies in one corner of the room and covered them with a plastic sheet. Fortunately it was air-conditioned; in the desert heat the corpses would decompose rapidly.

Now they were focused on the job at hand, Vance working on a laptop in the office while Ice chatted to a third man, an associate they had hired, a man that possessed a set of skills neither he nor Vance had.

Mitch Freeman had a background in aeronautical engineering and weapons development. The ultimate geek, he could fabricate almost anything and modify everything else. Having long left service in the British Defence Science and Technology Laboratory, he was now a contractor seeking thrills and adventure. The CIA officers had used him previously on a number of sensitive missions.

"Those nutjobs would've blown up half the bloody town," Mitch exclaimed as he examined the contents of the van with Ice. "There's three-quarters of a ton of bang in here."

"Yep," said Ice.

"You're lucky buggers, that's for sure." Mitch gave Ice a solid thump on the shoulder. Despite being a geek, the engineer sported a powerful frame, the result of hours lifting Olympic weights. It was his second great love after gadgets.

"I think we've got more than enough for two bombs," declared Ice.

"You might be right," Mitch agreed. "So that's the plan, yeah, two bombs. One in the van and one in the Land Cruiser?"

Vance walked out of the office and joined them. "That gonna be a problem, Mitch?"

"Nah, dead easy. How much time do I have?"

"Ah, that's the hard bit," said Vance. "Tariq just e-mailed me Hussein's movements for the next few days. We've got a small window tomorrow. That means you've got just under 24 hours to make all the mods."

"Not a problem, my good man. Not a problem at all."

Chapter Six

THE THREE ARMORED Mercedes swept out of the Presidential Palace at precisely 0700 hours. They left the Ras al-Akhdar peninsula with a police escort, speeding past the Emirates Palace hotel and the expensive foreshore developments. The escort cleared the morning traffic with wailing sirens and flashing lights.

Tariq's father, Sheik Hussein Ahmed, was in the first Mercedes. As security adviser to the emir, he preferred to travel with a police escort. It helped deal with the peak-hour traffic.

Hussein sat upright, watching the modern buildings. His features were emotionless, resembling an ancient statue battered and worn by the windswept desert. The white robes and kaffiyeh added to the likeness.

On the seat beside him sat Hussein's head of security, the man responsible for turning his evil intentions into outcomes.

"Have you heard from Yussuf?" asked Hussein.

"No. He will contact me once it is done. I gave him

strict orders to remain undercover until it is complete. He has never failed us before." The man checked his watch. "The bomb will go off today as planned."

"The Americans are still at the clinic? Even after my son chose to warn them?"

"Yes. I thought they might all flee, but two chose to remain."

Hussein continued to look out the window. "These two are CIA?"

"Yes, this is what my sources inform me. These Americans are arrogant; they think they can stop us. It will prove to be their downfall."

"Hmmm." Hussein returned his attention to the scenery outside the limousine as the convoy crossed the Mussafah Bridge. From the apex of the span he could make out the industrial sector, five kilometers away. He almost missed the distant flash and the angry black cloud that rolled up into the clear morning sky.

"*Allahu Akbar*," he whispered.

A few seconds later the Mercedes shuddered as the shock wave of the blast washed over it. Hussein's man snapped his eyes to the window, concern on his face. It took him a second to realize what had occurred.

"Impeccable timing," Hussein said with a cruel smile. His subordinate turned back to face him, eyes shining with excitement.

"Two less of Satan's puppets."

They were interrupted by the whine of an electric motor. The soundproof divider that separated them from the driver of the vehicle lowered. "Sir, there has been an explosion in the Mussafah industrial estate. Our escort is recommending we return to the palace for our own safety."

The security head looked to his boss, who shook his

head, smirking. "We will continue to the airport as planned."

Hussein waited for the divider to slot back in place before continuing. "I think the time has come to deal with my son."

"It is sad that Tariq does not join his father in jihad."

"He has been corrupted by the infidels and become one of them. We have watched him for long enough. Make the necessary arrangements."

The convoy continued to the airport, sirens wailing as it raced down the highway. On either side, palm trees and bushes flashed past, occasional gaps in the greenery revealing glimpses of the encroaching desert.

Six miles from the airport they swept under the 16th Street overpass. The police escort failed to notice the battered Toyota Land Cruiser accelerating down the ramp that joined the highway. It merged with the inside lane and continued to gather speed, gaining on the convoy.

Overtaking traffic, it edged toward them, lane by lane. The rearmost Mercedes broke formation, horn blaring, racing forward to position itself between the speeding four-wheel drive and Hussein's vehicle.

In the back of his car, Hussein was thrown to one side as the driver reacted. The codriver had the window down in a split second. The chatter of his submachine gun filled the interior of the car.

Bullets shattered the windshield of the Toyota; a figure at the wheel toppled sideways. Unaffected by the demise of the driver, the Land Cruiser continued to gain speed, engine screaming, flames belching from the exhaust pipe. It danced around a slow-moving truck, seemingly possessed.

Hussein had turned in his chair and watched in horror

as it swerved closer. "Faster! Faster!" he screamed as the codriver emptied another magazine into the rogue vehicle.

The four-wheel drive hit them with a crunch and detonated. Three hundred kilograms of military-grade explosives obliterated the Land Cruiser adding to the shrapnel. The armor on the Mercedes was designed to stop bullets, not a car bomb. The blast shredded metal and flesh, spreading the remains of Sheik Hussein Ahmed and his men over an area the size of a football field. A single burning tire from the Land Cruiser bounced down the road toward the airport.

Five miles away, in the business center of the Etihad Airways first-class lounge, Mitch Freeman closed his laptop. He disconnected the cell phone from its USB port and bundled the equipment into a leather satchel. Slinging the bag over his shoulder, he walked back through the lounge, past the concierge, and out into the main departure hall of the airport. He checked his ticket and strode quickly to the corresponding gate. Ice and Vance were waiting.

"We all good?" asked Vance.

"Tip-top, mate. Now let's get the hell out of here," replied Mitch.

The men handed their tickets to the waiting flight attendant. She gave them a curious look before smiling. "Have a lovely time in the Maldives, gentlemen."

Chapter Seven

THE MALDIVES

TWO WEEKS LATER, Lascar Logistics flight WMX334 touched down at Malé International Airport. The luxury Gulfstream G500 pulled onto the parking area reserved for private aircraft. A golf cart zoomed up to the jet as the door opened and the stairs lowered onto the runway.

"Welcome to the Maldives, Mr. Ahmed," a smiling official greeted Tariq at the cart. "Everything has been arranged."

"Thank you very much. Greatly appreciated." Tariq shook the man's hand and got into the cart. The debonair Arab was dressed in clothing that befitted the tropical climate: linen pants and a Hawaiian shirt, topped off by a white Panama hat.

They raced across the tarmac, pausing for a few seconds at the terminal door for another official to stamp Tariq's passport. Then it was a short run through the terminal, out across a road, and down onto a covered boardwalk.

A luxury motor cruiser was moored against the wharf. Its sleek lines and the deep throb of the idling engines gave the impression of speed and power. Tariq grabbed his leather bag and jumped onto the rear deck, giving the captain on the flybridge a wave. The Maldivian official cast off the lines and the marine engines roared as the craft eased away from the dock.

They cleared the breakwater within a few minutes, and once free of the marina speed limit, the captain opened the twin supercharged diesels up to full throttle. The sixty-foot cruiser leaped forward, the props churning the blue waters. Tariq grabbed at the railing and his hat flipped off his head into the clear sky. He smiled, the stresses of his father's funeral and the takeover of Lascar Logistics disappearing behind him.

The cruiser ate up the distance from Malé to the island resort in under an hour. Tariq had chosen the hideaway as it matched his criteria perfectly: small enough to book out, equipped with all the required comforts, and within an hour of an international airport.

One of the island's hosts greeted him with a broad smile as the boat bumped against the tires lashed to the jetty. Tariq threw his bag onto the weathered planks and followed the beaming Maldivian along the gangway and onto the sand.

The island was only a few hundred feet across, with brilliant white sands, palm trees, and a boutique villa in the center. It was paradise.

Tariq kicked off his loafers, enjoying the feel of the sand as he padded toward the villa. He ducked under some low-hanging palms and emerged to an outdoor bar and restaurant. Three men were lounging around a table in similar attire to Tariq. An ice chest filled with beers nestled in the sand next to them.

"Gentlemen, I hope you don't mind if I join you," asked Tariq.

The men stopped their conversation and turned to face him. A broad smile appeared on Vance's face as he realized who it was. "Tariq, good to see you, buddy."

Ice grabbed another chair, adding it to the table.

The third man, a muscular fellow sporting a bushy beard and a receding hairline, stood and offered Tariq a hand. "Mitch Freeman at your service."

Tariq grasped the British engineer's hand firmly. "It is a pleasure to meet you, Mitch Freeman. Vance tells me your skills were critical to our operation."

Mitch laughed. "Vance exaggerates, and the pleasure is all mine, or should I say *ours*. Your choice of location for this meeting is fantastic."

They had been on the island since the day of the Abu Dhabi bombings. Tariq had needed them to disappear, and what better place than an isolated tropical island, free from the prying eyes of investigators.

"I apologize for the wait," said Tariq, "but there have been many things for me to deal with."

Ice pulled a beer from the chest and popped the top on the edge of the table. "Oh, it's been hard, boss," he said, smiling.

"I say," Mitch added, "You two," he used his beer to point at the former CIA operatives, "have been drinking a shitload of booze. For a pair of dead chaps, that is."

They all laughed and Tariq eased himself into his chair.

Mitch's first bomb had torn apart the CIA 'medical clinic' and disintegrated the remains of the terrorists they had killed earlier. The only identifiable traces had been pieces of equipment, including the personal sidearms of two CIA officers. The agency had declared them killed in action.

"So what's the lowdown on the attack, Tariq?" Vance asked.

"Your plan worked perfectly. There were no traces of Mitch's remote-control kit, just pieces of the dead suicide bomber. Ironically, the police have attributed the attack to extremists and my father has been given a state funeral."

"If only they knew the truth," murmured Ice as he tipped a beer to his lips.

"And what about your father's empire?" asked Vance.

"It is now under my stewardship," answered Tariq.

"Good stuff. I love it when a plan comes together," said Vance, giving his best impression of Hannibal from *The A-Team*.

Tariq laughed. "You look more like Mr. T." The joke prompted grins from the rest of the team.

"So what now?" asked Ice seriously.

"Well, I'm afraid I can't stay for long, for there is much work to do." He had their undivided attention. "Your mission is to build an organization capable of dealing with men like my father—across the globe. Men who think they are above the law. Evil men who sow hatred and pain wherever they walk."

Vance nodded.

Tariq continued. "I want you to find these men and I want you to stop them."

He reached into his pocket and placed a USB drive on the table. "Vance, I mentioned that my father was running a department of Lascar Logistics as a front to channel funding to terrorists. It seems that I underestimated how much he had invested into Priority Movements Airlift. I can assure you that it is sufficient for our needs. That stick has all the account details and access codes for what I am calling the PRIMAL fund."

"PRIMAL. I like that," said Ice.

"Yeah, it rings true with me," added Mitch.

"Let me get this straight," asked Vance. "You want to fund us to run around the world whacking all those evil fuckers that the CIA never let us touch?"

"Not how I would have described it, but yes, that is the crux of the concept."

There was silence at the table as the three men considered Tariq's proposal.

Ice broke the silence. "I'm in."

Mitch followed suit. "Me too. I need a new job."

They both turned to Vance, who would head the operation.

"We would have full autonomy to select our targets and missions?" he asked.

"Of course," answered Tariq.

Vance took a swig of his beer. "Shit hot! Let's do it."

"Excellent." Tariq rose and shook their hands. He had confidence in this team. Vance was a natural leader and a man of strong moral fiber. Blunt, confronting, and audacious, he was the perfect commander. His partner, Ice, was calm, deadly, and meticulous. The type of operative who could achieve anything he set his mind to. This third individual, Mitch Freeman, was a genius. Someone who could make machines and technology dance at his fingertips.

"The three of you will have to lay low for a few more weeks. If you need to recruit additional personnel you can do so but stay clear of the Emirates. I'll send a plane for you when things have settled and I've secured a base of operations."

"Sounds good." Vance nodded.

"Now, my friends, I must return to Abu Dhabi."

"Already? No sleep for the wicked, eh?" asked Mitch.

"Not with PRIMAL lurking in the shadows." With that, Tariq disappeared behind the palms, heading back toward the wharf.

The three remaining men sat speechless. All of them had fantasized about running carte blanche on neutralizing bad guys. Having the opportunity thrust upon them, however, was slightly overwhelming.

Vance broke the silence, calling the waiter. "Paper and pens, please, Maurice." He turned back to his team. "Well, folks, better start planning. First things first, we're gonna need more men."

"I've got a few guys in mind," Ice said. "We definitely need a head of intel. Tracking down our targets is going to take real brains. I know this guy, Chua."

"Yeah, I know Chua. He's good," agreed Vance. "I'll drop him a call. I'm also thinking of another guy. Lunatic Aussie who goes by the name Bishop."

"You handle the lads, yeah, and I'll concentrate on the gear," Mitch added, picking up the USB drive on the table. "I'll need a line of credit because I'm guessing you will want a lot of kit."

"Damn straight," replied Vance. "If it flies, drives, shoots, finds, swims, explodes, or sings, then PRIMAL wants it. By the time we're ready to roll, I want to be able to reach out and touch any murdering, polluting, exploiting, fucktard on the face of the earth. We're gonna make Mossad and the CIA look like a bunch of cookie-selling Girl Scouts!"

Chapter Eight

CAMP SMITH, HAWAII

MAJOR CHEN CHUA of the US Army was walking out the door of his office at Camp Smith in Hawaii when he was stopped by one of his noncoms. "Sir, there's a phone call for you."

"Can you take a message? I'll get to it on Monday." The lightly-built Chinese American had planned to throw his mountain bike down one of the ridgelines behind Diamond Head.

"Sir, some guy called Vance insisted that I come out and get you; he said it was urgent."

Chua's interest piqued with the mention of his old CIA contact. He gave the bike perched on top of his Jeep a longing look and turned back into the SOCPAC intelligence facility.

He made his way into the building, swiped through two doors, and sat at his desk. "Major Chua speaking."

"Hey bud, it's Vance."

"You're supposed to be dead."

"That's no way to greet an old friend."

Chua looked down at the phone; the caller ID was blank and yet the call was still coming through on the encrypted military network.

"Vance, where are you calling from?"

"I'm on a beach under a palm tree. Look bud, I need to know if you're still looking for work?"

"Yes, I mean no. Discharge papers are in; I'm out in four weeks. I've taken a job working for British Petroleum."

"You're kidding me. You're hanging up your boots to work for those scumbags?"

"It's not as bad as it seems."

"Screw that, I've got a job for you here. Guaranteed twice the pay, and you won't feel like a blood-sucking corporate wiener."

"What's the catch? Do I have to die like you?"

"Pretty much, but sure as shit you won't regret it."

"Let me think about it." Chua reached into the minifridge under his desk and cracked a can of energy drink.

Vance heard the telltale hiss of the can opening. "That crud will kill you, Chua."

"My only vice. Now something tells me this wasn't just a recruiting call."

"You're onto me. I need you to find someone."

"Who?"

"Guy by the name of Aden Bishop. Ex–Australian Army intelligence."

"The Sierra Leone guy, right? The one who was court-martialed for saving a camp full of refugees?" Chua scribbled some notes on a pad.

"That's him. I know you guys work with the Aussies a lot, I need you to track Bishop down."

"You going to offer him a job too?"

"Not much gets past you, does it bud?"

"This is going to take me a few days."

"No problem; drop me an e-mail at vanceonvacation@gmail.com when you find him."

Chua laughed. "Will do. Any chance you're going to be in town in the future?"

"That depends."

"On what?"

"On how serious you are about coming to work with me."

―――――

THE MALDIVES

Three days after he had contacted the Army intelligence officer Vance had an e-mail in his inbox. He opened it on one of the laptops Mitch had set up with an untraceable satellite link to the internet.

"You're shitting me," he exclaimed as he read the message.

Mitch also had his laptop out on the table, working off the same link. "What's the go?"

"Chua found Bishop."

"Brilliant, so where is he?"

"Spain."

"Nice, I always liked Spain. Plenty of hot birds, lots of sun. Bit of a pants man your Bishop, is he?"

"Not exactly, he's there to bury his parents."

"What?"

"Yeah, listen to this." Vance read from the email. "The Department of Foreign Affairs and Trade has identified that two Australian nationals were killed in the terrorist attack on Israel Airlines flight LY395. M. and C. Bishop, from Sydney, were both listed on the manifest and are presumed dead. Of note: They were the parents of one A. Bishop, a former member of the Australian Defence Force."

"That's messed up."

"What's messed up?" asked Ice. The former marine was clad only in a pair of shorts; he had been training on the beach.

"Bishop, the guy Vance is trying to recruit. His parents were killed in that airliner that was shot down."

"No shit? The Israeli one?" Ice asked.

"Yeah," answered Vance. "Chua's located him in Valencia, Spain. The funeral's in two days."

"You going to go?" Ice asked.

"Yeah, I think I will."

"Not sure it's the most appropriate time to pitch a job, old man," said Mitch.

"You kidding me, terrorists have just killed his entire family. We're going to give him the opportunity to find and kill the bastards. I know Bishop, this is exactly what he'll be looking for." Vance picked up the satellite phone. "I'll be gone a few days at most. You two stay out of trouble."

"We're on a desert island with cold beer and no women," said Ice. "How much trouble do you think we can get into?"

Chapter Nine

DUBAI

THE ARAB DESERT Construction building site was on the outskirts of Dubai. In the early stages of construction, it consisted of a concrete foundation laid over the desert and the first levels of scaffolding. Over the next six months it would transform into a five-star resort. An army of foreign workers, Pakistani, Bangladeshi, and Indian, would labor around the clock to take it from bare sand to a sparkling jewel on the shores of the Arabian Gulf.

The sun peeked over the desert horizon as the morning shift of workers arrived, transported from their accommodation in an old school bus. It looked like something from an apocalyptic movie set; bars welded across the bus windows to dissuade any attempt to seek alternative employment. Floodlights illuminated the men as they disembarked. Towels and torn blankets were wrapped tight around their wiry bodies to ward off the frigid night air.

One by one they marched off the bus and shuffled toward their work areas.

Once the bus was empty the off-going shift stumbled onto it like zombies. Exhausted from twelve hours of hard labor, they collapsed onto the hard benches, many falling asleep almost immediately.

A team of muscled enforcers and a stern-faced foreman oversaw the shift change. They carried wooden clubs and long sticks to help motivate the workers. Mostly Russian, they had been selected for their brutality.

Maruf was a sixteen-year-old immigrant from Pakistan. He had been in Dubai for six long months. Since his arrival he'd realized that the opportunity presented by the recruiting office in Karachi was not as it seemed. He had been beaten, his passport confiscated, wages halved, and his life threatened by the Russian gangsters who ran Arab Desert Construction.

"What are you doing?" One of the enforcers pointed his club at Maruf as the skinny teenager leaned against the scaffolding, fighting for breath. He had finished carrying a forty-pound bag of concrete up a rickety staircase to the second level and was regaining his energy as he caught a glimpse of the sunrise.

"Working, sir, working." He turned and ran down the stairs. Under the cold eyes of the Russian thug he hefted another bag onto his shoulder and made his way back up.

As he neared the top he felt something give way. He reached out and grabbed one of the uprights, steadying himself. The pole swayed outward with a creak. He lost grip on the bag and it dropped, hitting the wooden stairs. There was an almighty crack, and Maruf and the bag fell through, hitting the ground with a crash. The entire scaffolding toppled sideways, collapsing into a heap.

It took the workers a few minutes to pull the slight Pakistani from under the wreckage.

"You stupid shit, you brought down half the site." The enforcer stood over Maruf's battered body, his wooden club in hand. "Take him over to the office. The rest of you fix this mess up," he said with a thick Slavic accent.

Four laborers grasped a limb each and carried the stunned boy toward the site office. As they crossed an access track a truck pulled into the construction site.

The Toyota Land Cruiser had a logo emblazoned on the door: two *L*'s facing each other and the words *Lascar Logistics*. It pulled up next to the office and a dark-skinned man wearing a Lascar polo-shirt climbed out of the cabin. He took a package from the passenger seat and walked it into the office.

The four workers placed Maruf in the sand alongside the demountable building. Three of them fled back to their work. One stayed to see if the boy was badly injured.

"Get back to work!" the enforcer screamed at him.

The man fled and Maruf struggled to get to his feet. His arm was held across his chest, his face scrunched in pain.

"Not you, you idiot. You've set us back by days, cost us thousands of dollars. Someone has to pay for that."

The laborers had seen it happen before. Men beaten to death for less. Others so badly injured they were left crippled, beggars in the camps. They all looked away, terrified of drawing any attention to themselves.

The Russian stood over Maruf with his club raised. There was a look of pure terror on the injured boy's face.

"Stop! What are you doing?" The Lascar Logistics employee, an Indian, stood in the door of the office. "This man is badly injured, he needs medical aid." He stepped off the transportable building's wooden deck and made his way toward Maruf.

"Fuck off and mind your own business," the Russian snarled.

"Leave him alone." The Indian was half the size of the man he faced. "If you touch him I'm going to report you to the police."

"You wouldn't fucking dare." The Russian pulled back his jacket. The sun was now fully over the horizon and there was enough light to see the pistol jammed in his belt.

"Matra, you imbecile, put that away." Another overseer had appeared in the office doorway. He was tall, with gray eyes, short brown hair, and a hard, thin mouth. "Can't you see the man is injured? Take him to the infirmary." He turned to the Lascar Logistics driver. "I apologize for my man. He can be a little short-tempered sometimes."

Matra gave his boss a nod as he helped Maruf to his feet. They disappeared around the corner of the building.

The Lascar Logistics driver looked at the supervisor with suspicion. "I should be going."

"It's OK, I promise nothing will happen to the boy." The man smiled and thrust out his hand. "My name is Simeon. I'm sorry for the actions of my colleague; he can be overzealous at times."

The Indian nodded and shook the man's hand.

"Come, you can see for yourself."

"No, I need to get back to work." He edged toward his truck.

"No, no, I insist. Come see our medical facility. I don't want you thinking that we treat our workers bad. Of all the companies, we treat them the best." Simeon put his hand on the smaller man's shoulder and guided him around the corner.

Two rows of shipping containers with a corridor between them housed the building site's tools and materials. "Our infirmary is at the end. We have a nurse and everything," Simeon explained as they walked into the corridor.

The Lascar employee knew he'd made a fatal mistake when they passed the last container.

The enforcer was standing over Maruf's crumpled body, clothes speckled in blood and gore, club dripping scarlet. The teenage worker's face was an unrecognizable bloodied pulp.

"No, no," the Indian said with wide eyes.

"Oh yes, you stupid brown monkey." Matra grabbed him and wrapped a powerful forearm around his neck. "I'll teach you to stick your nose in where it's not wanted."

A thin stiletto blade punctured the man's lower back as he struggled against the headlock. It twisted upward, searching for vital organs. The tip ground against the Indian's spine and he convulsed. Blood dribbled from his mouth as his life ebbed away.

Simeon Isayev, the head of the Karelin mafia family's Dubai-based operation, watched with impassive features. "Bury them in the desert."

"Yes, boss." The enforcer grinned as he wiped the stiletto blade clean on the dead man's pant leg.

"Make sure you get rid of the truck."

Chapter Ten

THE MALDIVES

THE SATELLITE PHONE buzzed its way across the table like a crazed insect. It was Ice who reached for it, putting down the tablet he was reading from. He answered the call, listened for a few seconds, then dropped the phone back on the table. "It's Vance, he's ten minutes out. Got the new guy with him."

Mitch looked up from his laptop. "Probably be a good idea to head down to the dock and welcome him, what do you say?"

"Yeah."

Ice grabbed two beers from the chest and they set off through the palm trees toward the island's short jetty.

"You keen for a dive later?" Mitch asked.

"Yeah, we might take the new guy."

"Good plan."

They reached the wharf as the high-powered cruiser bumped up against it. Grabbing the lines thrown by the skipper, they held the boat tight as Vance and Bishop leaped onto the wharf with their bags.

"Aden Bishop, I'd like you to meet Mitch and Ice." Vance made the introduction with a sweep of his arm.

The newcomer was medium build, around five eleven, and wore a tired smile. He had the kind of rugged looks that you would see in a TV commercial for four-wheel drives or gardening equipment: an unruly mop of brown hair, strong jaw, and nose that had been broken more than once.

"G'day, pleasure to meet you both." Bishop extended a hand to both men.

"Thought you might like a refresher." Ice handed him a cold beer.

"Nice one." Bishop smiled, took the Corona, and examined it. "What, no real beer?" he joked.

"I'm afraid we're all out. I could get you a Bud Light if that's more your style."

"I'll leave the lolly water for you Yanks."

"As long as it's not Foster's, I'm happy." Mitch smiled. "Not that keen on convict swill."

They all laughed except for Vance. "So, no one brought me a mojito?"

"Negative, boss, we're all out of rum." Ice picked up one of Bishop's bags and led them back along the jetty, over fine white sand, and into the resort.

"Welcome to our humble home," said Mitch as they all pulled up chairs around a table.

"Not for much longer." Vance selected a beer from the ice chest.

"What's the go?" asked Ice. "Has Tariq found us something more permanent?"

"It would seem that way. I got the feeling there's something on the boil and he wants us close."

"More of his evil relatives?" said Mitch.

"No, I don't know what's going on, but he's stockpiled a lot of the gear you ordered."

"When are we off?" Bishop asked. "Should I bother unpacking?"

"It'll be a few more days at least."

"Plenty of time to get in another dive," exclaimed Ice. "Bish, you in?"

The Australian took a long pull from his beer. "Yeah, sounds good."

"Get it in while you can, boys. Something tells me that when we get back into the UAE we're going to be pretty damn busy."

———

ABU DHABI

Lascar Logistics' headquarters was perched on the top floor of one of the many high-rises dominating Abu Dhabi's skyline. From behind his desk Tariq could look out through the floor-to-ceiling windows and take in the expanse of the Arabian Gulf.

"Mr. Ahmed, there is a Major Mohammed Al Shamsi here to see you." The assistant's voice came over the intercom on the desk.

"Send him in." Tariq stood and smoothed out the creases in his pants. He put his jacket on and walked across to the door.

There was a knock and he opened it. *"As-salaam alaykum,"* he greeted his guest with a broad smile.

"*Wa-alaykum salaam*," responded the khaki-clad policeman.

"Please come, take a seat, my friend," Tariq continued in Arabic, guiding the man to a pair of leather chesterfields in the corner of his office.

"You have come a long way from Special Branch, Tariq," said Mohammed as he sat on the couch. "The view from your old office was nice, but this is spectacular. I just wish it had happened under better circumstances."

"The loss of my father was tragic and has overshadowed everything this last month."

"Once again, my condolences."

"Thank you, my brother. Perhaps you would like a refreshment."

"No, I am fine." He placed his cap down on the coffee table. "I'm afraid that I bring bad news."

"Go on." Tariq sat in the chair opposite.

"We found your missing man. He was murdered."

"How? Where?"

"His body and the body of another man were found in the desert. Someone had made a poor attempt at burying them. His truck was located a few kilometers away, burnt out. The police working the case think he was set upon by a gang of marauding laborers."

"Laborers?"

"Yes, there have been reports that some of the Pakistanis and Indians have formed a gang and have been hijacking cars."

"That's interesting. I was not aware of such a thing."

The policeman shrugged. "Desperate people do desperate things."

"So they have closed the case?"

"Yes, they have."

"That's interesting. I wonder why a group of marauding laborers would kill one of their own."

"What do you mean?"

"The man who went missing was an Indian national. My company offered him employment after he fled a construction company that was attempting to blackmail him."

The police officer was silent.

"Mohammed, we have been friends for a long time. Tell me the real reason the police have closed this case. Tell me why they will not pursue justice for one of my workers." Tariq's cold green eyes locked with the policeman's.

"Well, we backtracked your man to his last known location. A construction company called Arab Desert Construction. According to their chief of operations he made the delivery and left."

"I was aware of his last delivery, go on."

"When I started to dig into the background of this Arab Desert Construction I hit a wall. I was sent an e-mail direct from the Chief of Police's office informing me I was off the case. It was reassigned to another branch and subsequently closed."

"So Arab Desert Construction has friends in high places."

"It would seem so."

Tariq stared at the policeman for a moment. "Then I guess this is where it ends."

Mohammed nodded. "I think that is best. Even with your connections, investigating this further is only going to cause more problems. Justice will not bring back your man, it will only endanger the lives of others."

"I agree. Thank you for your help, brother."

"It is my honor." Mohammed picked up his cap and stood out of the chair.

Tariq smiled as they shook hands. "How is your family?"

"Very good. My wife told me to tell you that she has found you a suitable wife."

Tariq laughed as they walked to the office door. "I'm sure she has. Another one of her cousins, no doubt."

"One of these days she will find one to your liking."

"I can only hope. Take care, my friend."

Tariq closed the doors behind the policeman and returned to his desk. He reached into one of the drawers and removed a secure satellite phone. He had a mission for **PRIMAL**.

Chapter Eleven

PRIORITY MOVEMENTS AIRLIFT HANGAR, ABU
DHABI INTERNATIONAL AIRPORT

"WELCOME TO YOUR NEW HOME, GENTLEMEN." Tariq
was waiting inside the hangar when they arrived.

The team of four had taken a Lascar flight from the
Maldives direct to Abu Dhabi International Airport. They
had pulled into a Lascar Logistics bay only a few hundred
feet from the hangar. It was a short walk even dragging their
gear bags.

"Ice, Mitch, I see you've been taking full advantage of
the weather in the Maldives." Both were sporting healthy
tans. "You must be Aden." Tariq shook the Australian's
hand. "Vance has told me a lot about you. It is a pleasure to
have you on the team."

"Sir, the pleasure is all mine."

"So what do you think?" Tariq gestured to the recently
renovated facility.

"It's perfect," replied Vance.

55

The hangar was big enough to house a 747. Only one aircraft was inside, a sleek Gulfstream business jet that was dwarfed by the cavernous space. Across from the jet the hangar had been converted into living quarters with individual rooms, a recreation and operations room, kitchen, and an armory. In the back corner was a basic gym, complete with Olympic bars, a rowing machine, chin-up bar, and ropes that hung from the ceiling. Next to the gym were parked two black Mercedes SUVs with official license plates.

"Mitch, this is the access code and swipe card for the armory." Tariq handed him an envelope and pointed out a block of shipping containers. "You should find everything you have ordered in there."

"Brilliant, I'll check it out." PRIMAL's science and technology guru walked over to the battered containers. They had been welded together and modified with a sophisticated security door. He opened it with the card and access code then turned on the lights.

The outside may have looked worn but inside was a different story; the armory was immaculate. One side of the room was covered in mesh and had weapons hung on it, an impressive selection ranging from compact pistols through to machine guns and sniper rifles. The other side was a geek's wet dream; it had a workbench, mini-lathe, CNC machine, 3D printer, tool boxes, and high-powered computers. He sat on a swivel chair and surveyed the room with a smile. A bang on the side of the container brought him back to reality. He opened the door and stuck his head out.

"Nice of you to join us," said Vance. "You happy with all your whizbangs, bud?"

"Ace," Mitch confirmed with a thumbs-up.

"Good, what about that?" Vance asked, pointing at the Gulfstream. "Can you fly it?"

"Sure can, old man."

Vance turned back to Tariq. "I think we've got everything we'll need."

"If you think of anything else, just ask."

"There's only one other thing."

"Yes."

"The mission. What is it?"

"Of course, I'll brief you all now."

The team gathered in the operations and planning room. With its high-fidelity projector and surround-sound system, it doubled as a recreation facility. Once they were seated Tariq updated them on the situation regarding his murdered employee and the subsequent police response.

"Have you got any more information on these Arab Desert Construction guys?" Vance asked.

"Here's the whole police file." Tariq took a bundle of documents from his leather satchel. "They're Russian mafia."

"Oh tip-top, my favorite kind of Russian," said Mitch. "One who would sell his own mother and cut the throat of his brother."

"Yes, they're ruthless and have got some powerful friends. Managed to stonewall the investigation into my employee's death despite my own attempts to get to the bottom of it." He passed the file to Vance. "Unfortunately this file is limited. It fails to identify which mafia family we are dealing with. I suspect they may have bought their way out of the police records."

"They've got deep pockets then; nothing comes cheap in this town." Vance flicked through the pages in the file. "So what's the mission? You want us to take these guys down?"

"Yes, I want this syndicate out of the Emirates and I want the men responsible for the death of my employee punished. The suffering they have caused needs to cease."

"Got it." Vance's nose was buried in the file. "According to this, ADC has a labor camp located outside of Dubai. That looks like a good place to start."

"I will leave you to it then." Tariq rose from the table, gave a nod, and left.

"Mitch, how are we for tech?" Vance asked. "Can you whip up some credentials for Bishop and Ice?"

"With what I've got in that tin can, it shouldn't be a problem."

"Good, let's get to work. By close of business tomorrow I want to know who we're dealing with and how to stop them."

Chapter Twelve

ADC MIGRANT WORKER CAMP, DUBAI

THE SUV TURNED off the highway fifteen miles outside of Dubai and bounced along a potholed road as it followed the high fence surrounding the workers' camp. The landscape was devoid of vegetation; desert surrounded the endless rows of disheveled transportable buildings.

"So this is where Arab Desert Construction keeps all their laborers?" Bishop said as he drove.

"Yeah," replied Ice. "According to their pamphlet it houses fifteen hundred workers in comfortable living arrangements."

"Ten bucks says it's bullshit and the poor bastards are jammed in like cattle. I've seen camps like this before." They pulled off the asphalt and stopped at the camp entrance. A set of heavy gates barred the way. To the side was a makeshift guardbox.

Bishop honked the horn. There was no sign of movement. "No one's home." They jumped out and walked over to the building. Ice gave the door a solid rap with his knuckles.

A moment later it opened and an overweight Arab dressed in a security uniform appeared. He gave the pair the once-over; both men were wearing aviator sunglasses and loose-fitting short-sleeve shirts and slacks. "What do you want?"

"Hi, we're from the Human Rights Watch, just wanted to have a look around," said Bishop with a smile. He took his forged credentials from his pocket and showed them to the guard.

The guard frowned. His obese features scrunched up, making him look like a boxer dog. "I don't think you're allowed in here."

"You don't think?" Bishop said. "This is accommodation for immigrant workers, not a prison. We're in the process of doing inspections on a number of locations."

The man looked confused. "I need to check with—"

"No, you don't!" Bishop said, raising his voice and pulling out his phone. "You need to open that goddamn gate before I ring the Chief of Police and have you charged with denying civil liberties."

Ice looked down at the guard from his six foot five inches and frowned. The guard's face scrunched up even more. "You can't take your car in," he muttered.

"That's fine. We'll leave it here with you." Bishop gave a smile.

The Arab nodded, happy for a win. He waddled across to the gate and unlocked it.

The PRIMAL operatives squeezed through. The guard locked the gate behind them and shuffled back to his office.

"Helpful fellow," said Bishop.

"Nice one, bro. I don't think he knew what hit him."

"How long do you give it 'til the Russians rock up? Ten, fifteen minutes?"

"I'd say longer. They don't like the heat."

"Neither do I." Bishop wiped the sweat under the brim of his Yankees cap and glanced at his watch. It was only 0900 hours and it already felt 110 degrees. It was going to be a scorcher.

They walked two hundred yards down the camp's main road toward the rows of single-story-accommodation buildings. Fine dust, pulverized by the wheels of buses, kicked up as they walked, covering their boots and pant legs.

"What a dump!" Bishop exclaimed as the smell of the camp hit their noses. "Clearly the plumbing doesn't work." Raw sewage filled the drains on either side of the track. The buildings were badly in need of repair; cardboard and plastic had been used to patch holes in the thin walls and cover broken windows. The place looked like a ghost town. There were no workers to be seen, clotheslines strung with laundry the only evidence of habitation.

They left the main road, carefully stepped over the effluent-filled drain, and moved between the tightly-packed transportable buildings. Faces appeared at windows as they walked, ducking under clotheslines and avoiding piles of trash. They never saw any women. All the faces at the windows were gaunt men with haunted eyes.

"They're all defeated," Ice said. "Utterly and totally defeated. Look at their eyes. This is no way for men to live."

"Like bloody POWs in a concentration camp."

Eventually they spotted a group outside, sitting in front of a building. The laborers watched them uneasily.

"Good morning. I was wondering if any of you know this man?" Bishop held out a photo of the murdered Lascar

Logistics employee. The workers glanced at the photo and shook their heads.

"We're trying to find anyone who might have seen him."

The men stood and began moving away.

"Where are you going?" asked Ice as they disappeared into the hut. "You've seen this man, haven't you?"

"They're terrified," said Bishop.

"Let's keep walking."

Further into the camp was the same story; desperation written on the faces of young and old men alike. They showed the picture to group after group, always getting the same result. A scared look and a shake of the head.

"Bish, we're getting nowhere with this."

"Yeah, maybe we should squeeze what we can out of Chief Wiggum at the front gate and call it a day."

"Sounds like a plan."

They angled back toward the main road, showing the photo to anyone they passed. Ice interrupted a game of cards to show it to some younger men. Four blank looks later they continued on their way.

"Ice, do you get the feeling we're being followed?" Bishop said quietly as they walked between the rows of huts.

"Sure do. Little guy is tailing us, has been for a few minutes now."

"You want to pick him up?"

"Probably better if you do it. I stick out a little."

"Roger." Bishop waited until they pushed through a patch of washing hanging from a line. He jogged ahead of Ice and ducked off to one side.

Ice kept walking, and a few seconds later their tail followed, slipping between the drying garments like a shadow.

Bishop moved in behind the young man, grabbed him

by the shoulder, and put him in a sleeper hold. "Don't struggle; I won't hurt you."

The boy's hands pried at Bishop's forearm, a futile effort as he was outweighed by at least forty pounds.

"I'm going to let you go, but if you try to escape I'll hurt you," Bishop whispered into the boy's ear. As he eased his grip Ice appeared. The frail immigrant worker gulped as he took in the size of the former Marine.

"Why were you following us?" Bishop asked.

Like the rest of the workers the youth was South Asian, dark-skinned, and malnourished. Bishop guessed he was probably a Bangladeshi. "The photo," the boy said softly.

Bishop held it out and the boy took it with a trembling hand. He studied it with intelligent eyes. "I know this man."

"Where did you see him?" Bishop asked.

"At the resort. He tried to save Maruf." Tears ran down the boy's cheeks. He wiped them away with a grubby hand. "They killed him."

"Who?"

"The Russians," the boy replied with a trembling voice.

"Which Russians? Do you know any names?" Bishop asked gently.

"Yes, the boss, his name is Simeon."

"Where do we find Simeon?"

"I have to go." The boy turned to run and Bishop grabbed him by the arm.

"Let me go; there are other people in the camp who will talk. The Russians will kill me."

Bishop took a handful of crumpled dollars and stuffed them into the boy's hand as he released him. The youth gave him a grateful look and disappeared around a corner.

"Now we've got a name," Ice said as he started off toward the road.

"Yeah, Simeon. Sounds like a nasty piece of work considering how shit-scared that kid was."

They reached the edge of the dwellings, jumped over the sewage ditch, and headed back toward the front gate. They had only gone a hundred yards when they heard the sound of a vehicle approaching.

"Here we go," Ice murmured.

"Hopefully we get to meet Simeon."

The Mercedes ML500 pulled up behind them. "Hey you, stop!" a voice yelled in heavily-accented English.

Bishop and Ice stopped and turned. Four men stepped out of the SUV, all solidly built, all wearing jeans, T-shirts, and, despite the heat, leather jackets.

"Hi." Bishop gave them a wave.

"What the fuck are you doing here?" asked one of the thugs. He had a shaved head and looked like his diet consisted mainly of horse steroids.

"I'm sorry, didn't your man at the gate tell you? We're from Human Rights Watch, just doing an inspection on the conditions of the camp."

"Who gave you permission to do that?"

"Oh I can't remember, some guy from your office." He looked at Ice. "Do you remember his name? I think it was 'Simon' or something."

Ice didn't miss a beat. "I seem to remember it was Simeon. Yeah, Simeon."

"Simeon Isayev?" The man looked surprised. "Simeon Isayev gave you permission to come here?" The other henchmen glanced at each other.

"Yes, that's correct." Bishop smiled. "Lovely fellow."

"I don't believe you. I'm going to call him."

"There's really no need."

"Shut your mouth." The thug started to dial a number on his cell phone.

Bishop pulled out his false credentials. "Simeon was nice enough to give us this letter. Do you want to see it?" He stepped forward, offering the document.

The Russian grunted. He had his phone to his ear with one hand and held out the other.

Bishop king-hit him square on the jaw, sending him reeling backward. The phone dropped onto the road.

One of his companions jumped into action, swinging a blow of his own. Bishop blocked the haymaker and counter-punched. His knuckles found the bigger man's ribs, knocking the wind out of him.

Ice snapped a kick that caught one of the other Russians in the groin. The man collapsed with a scream and Ice moved on to the last man standing. The mafia henchman managed to pull a pistol from his pants. He thumbed off the safety as Ice grasped the weapon, pulled it in under his arm, and lashed out with his opposite elbow, dropping the man like a sack of potatoes.

Meanwhile, Bishop's tussle with his second opponent had evolved into a ground fight. They were rolling in the dust until Bishop became pinned under the bigger man, his arms frantically blocking a rain of blows.

Ice grasped the Makarov pistol he'd taken from his opponent and smashed the grip into Bishop's wrestling partner's head. The Russian's eyes rolled up into his skull and he collapsed sideways, unconscious.

"Thanks, mate."

"Not a problem. Next time a little more warning would be nice." He offered Bishop a hand.

"Sure thing. I tend to get a little caught up in the moment sometimes." He dusted the dirt from his pants.

Two of the Russians were out cold. One was nursing his testicles and the leader was groggily trying to regain his feet.

Bishop drew the pistol Mitch had provided him. It was a compact USP .45. He retrieved a suppressor from his pants pocket and screwed it on.

"Where do I find Simeon Isayev?" He pointed the weapon directly at the leader's face.

"Fuck you!" the man slurred, his jaw broken.

The pistol snapped and the Russian screamed as the heavy slug tore through his kneecap. He collapsed to the ground.

Ice had his own pistol raised and was covering the other men.

"You've got another knee, then I start on the elbows. We can do this all day," said Bishop.

"He's at the office; it's in the industrial area," the man whimpered.

"What's the address?"

The Russian rattled it off.

"How many men?"

"Enough to kill you and your fucking boyfriend."

"More than four then," sneered Bishop.

The Russian glanced at the phone he had dropped and started laughing. "He knows you're coming, you dumb bastards."

Bishop picked up the cell phone. He checked the screen; it was still connected.

"Hello, Simeon, I'm very much looking forward to meeting you."

"Who the fuck is this, do you—"

"Any chance I could make an appointment and drop by this afternoon?" Bishop interrupted.

"Do you know who you're talking to? You're a fucking dead man."

"There's really no need for that aggression, Mr. Isayev. Human Rights Watch is a not-for-profit organization. We simply want to interview you about employee living conditions." Bishop looked out toward the camp. He could see faces peering out of the windows of the huts.

"Get fucked, you come near me and I'll see your corpse hanging from the rafters."

"Look, I'll drop by this afternoon, OK? I look forward to our chat." Bishop terminated the call and dropped the phone in his pocket. Out of the corner of his eye he caught a glimpse of the Russian's hand sliding into his jacket.

Bishop's .45 fired with a dull thud and the thug's head snapped back. He fell sideways, his jacket falling open to reveal a pistol tucked into a shoulder holster.

"These guys are pretty serious, bro," said Ice as he collected pistols from the remaining men and threw them into the sewage-filled ditch.

"Yeah, we'd better pack a little more heat for our meeting with Simeon." Bishop looked around for more henchmen. "C'mon, let's hit the road."

They started jogging to the front gate.

"Is it wrong that I'm really looking forward to meeting this Simeon guy?" said Bishop.

"Not at all."

"I knew we'd get along."

As they ran Ice dialed a number in his phone. "Mitch, it's Ice. We've got an address for you."

Chapter Thirteen

ADC OFFICE, DUBAI

"WHO THE FUCK ARE THESE PEOPLE?" Simeon yelled at the top of his lungs. The Arab security guard on the other end of the phone kept babbling about inspections so he threw the handset as hard as he could. It smashed through the glass panel in his door and landed on the carpet in front of his secretary. The pretty blonde picked it up and put it on her desk.

The Mafia lieutenant turned his attention to the wall, punching his fist clean through the drywall. "They arrived at the camp, told the guard they were fucking Human Watch or some shit. Then they killed Yakov and beat the shit out of everyone else. That fat, useless-prick guard. What the fuck would he know!"

Matra, the enforcer who had beaten Maruf to death, was standing in the corner of the room with his arms folded. "Maybe they are undercover police trying to find out more about that Lascar guy."

Simeon rolled his eyes. "Why is everyone so damn stupid? They were white—the police here don't hire white boys to do their heavy work. This is someone trying to flex their muscles. You watch, they are going to try to make demands of us."

"Who? No one except us is white."

"Someone could have hired mercenaries or some shit." Simeon opened his drawer, took out a Škorpion machine pistol, and placed it on the desk.

"Do you want me to go to the camp and find out if anyone knows anything?" Matra asked.

"No, you dumb ox, that fucker on the phone said he was coming to see us. I want you to stay right here and when he arrives I want you to shoot him in the face."

"Sir," the receptionist knocked on the door.

"What do you want?"

"The other men have arrived."

"Good, now let's see the look on this motherfucker's face when he turns up to my surprise party." He picked up the machine pistol and headed for the door.

———

"WHAT A SHITHOLE." Mitch was sitting in a battered Toyota Corolla on the street opposite the offices of Arab Desert Construction.

The building was part of a large fenced-off compound in the suburb of Muhaisnah. Like most of the structures in the area it was three stories high and constructed out of rendered concrete. Row after row of air conditioners jutted from the windows on each floor. At the front, vehicles were parked in a row. Nowhere was there a sign indicating it belonged to a construction company.

"Keeping it pretty low-key," said Mitch to himself. He reached over and turned up the air-conditioning. The *kaffiyeh* he was wearing was drenched in sweat.

The compound's steel gates swung open and a workman's van drove in and parked next to the other vehicles. The door slid open and a pack of thugs climbed out. Mitch caught a glimpse of an assault rifle. "Bingo."

His cell phone was sitting in his lap, a hands-free cable running to his ear. He hit one of the speed-dial buttons and it rang twice before Vance picked up. "Boss, this looks like the place. I just got a visual on four more heavies on target; looks like they're packing at least one AK. They're probably going to be ready for you."

"Do they look Russian?" Vance did not sound concerned.

"Big, shaved heads, jeans, and T-shirts. Yeah, old man, I'd say they're Russian mafia. I mean they're not wearing Cossack outfits, but hey, it's the next best thing."

"OK, smartass, we're a few minutes out. Give us any updates as you see fit."

"Roger, Mitch out."

———

"YOU SURE THIS Simeon guy will be there?" Vance asked from the backseat as they sped along a multi-lane highway in one of their new Mercedes SUVs. Ice was driving with Bishop in the passenger seat.

"Yeah, he'll be waiting," Bishop replied. "But he won't be expecting the shitstorm we're bringing."

All three PRIMAL operatives wore blue coveralls wrapped in assault body armor covered with pouches. Suppressed short-barrelled M4s hung from slings and

Bishop also had a compact shotgun resting across his knees. Ice wore a backpack, pressed up against the car seat.

"What's in the bag, Ice?" asked Vance.

"Some gear I thought we might need."

"Bish, the upside to having a former Marine on your team is you're never short on bang!"

Ice slowed as they approached the target address, the SUVs dark tinted windows keeping them hidden from view.

"That's it," said Bishop. "I can see Mitch's car."

Ice pulled over. "Everyone ready?" he asked as he pulled his Nomex balaclava on, adjusted his Oakleys, and activated his hearing protection.

Bishop followed suit, then drew back the bolt on his M4 a few millimeters to check that the first round was seated fully. "Ready."

In the back Vance ran through his own checks. "Good to go."

Fully kitted up with identical rigs, the three PRIMAL operatives could almost have passed for a police SWAT team.

Ice pushed down on the accelerator and the big V8 growled, launching them forward. Bishop felt a burst of adrenaline surge through his body.

The SUV bounced over the curb and its steel bullbar crashed through the gates to the compound. Ice brought it to a sliding halt in front of the office building. Bishop was out first, the shotgun in his shoulder. He aimed to the side of the door handle and fired.

The buckshot tore the lock from the door. Bishop pumped the shotgun and gave it another blast for good measure. Then he drove the barrel into the wood, pushing the shattered door open.

Ice lobbed in a flashbang. It detonated with a thump and he pushed inside, holding his M4 ready.

Inside the lobby a man lay on the floor, an AK assault rifle by his side. He moaned with hands clamped over his ears, eyes tightly shut. Ice kicked the AK away and covered the stairs. Vance was next in; he took up a position to the left of Ice covering the ground-floor doors.

Bishop entered last, the shotgun hanging from its sling. He took a pair of zip-ties from his vest and secured the shocked gunman.

A deafening volley of shots splintered the door in front of Vance, narrowly missing his head. He blasted the door with a long burst from his M4 then kicked it open. The bullet-riddled corpse of another mobster twitched on the floor.

Vance and Bishop worked as a team to clear the rest of the bottom floor. Once they'd made sure there were no more threats lurking in the other rooms they joined Ice back at the stairs.

Ice gave them a hand signal as he covered the stairs, indicating at least three more were on the upper floor.

"How we going to do this?" Bishop asked.

"We could always bring a few of them down to us," said Ice.

"I like that idea. Let's make it happen," said Vance.

Ice took less than a minute to prepare his charges. He dragged a table across to the middle of one of the rooms and used it to reach the ceiling. He smashed the drywall from the roof with the butt of his M4 and taped the two pounds of semtex directly to the concrete. Once he was done he activated the fuse and moved back to the stairs.

"Five, four, three, two, one," he counted.

The explosion was deafening and reverberated throughout the building. It fractured the entire floor of one of the upstairs rooms, causing it to collapse.

Bishop and Vance used the explosion as a distraction. They charged up the stairs and caught two gunmen cold in an office. They cut them down in a hail of gunfire.

Ice waited for the dust to settle before he rushed back into the room with the collapsed ceiling. There were two men lying in the rubble, covered in debris. One of them clutched a pistol. Ice shot him through the head. The other man struggled to get to his feet and Ice knocked him out with a swift kick to the face.

Back up on the upper floor a woman screamed from under a desk.

"Hey, it's OK. We're not going to hurt you." Bishop offered her a hand and helped her up.

"All clear." Vance appeared from one of the side rooms.

The woman's eyes were wide with fear as she stared at the balaclava-wearing intruders.

"Keep an eye on her." Bishop pushed open the door to the main office. Inside, the floor was completely missing. He could see down to where Ice was securing the hands of one of the Russians behind his back. Unlike the others, this man was of average build, and dressed conservatively with a suit jacket and slacks. "Vance, bring her here." He waited until the woman was standing next to him. "Who's that?" he pointed at the man Ice had captured.

She looked down into the rubble. "Simeon," she whispered. "That's Simeon."

———

PRIORITY MOVEMENTS AIRLIFT HANGAR

Vance strode into the shipping container and the door slammed shut. He adjusted the mouth of his balaclava before approaching their prisoner.

"It's a pleasure to meet you, Mr. Simeon Isayev."

The Mafia lieutenant wore a black hood and was tied to a chair. He squinted as Vance ripped the hood off. Harsh fluorescent lights illuminated the otherwise empty container.

"Where am I?" Simeon shook his head in an attempt to clear the grogginess.

"Somewhere no one can hear you scream."

"Do you know who I am?" the Russian snarled. "If you don't free me immediately some very powerful people will come looking for you."

"Your threats mean nothing. You're a low-level gang banger. I could put a bullet in your head, dump you in a ditch, and no one would give lesser of a fuck."

Simeon contemplated that thought, his eyes darting around the container as he searched for an opportunity to escape. At the same time he wriggled his hands against the zip ties. They were ruthlessly tight.

"You've got nothing to bargain with, Mr. Isayev. Nothing at all."

"Then why am I still alive?"

"Because I want you to deliver a message to your boss."

"Fuck you, deliver your own message."

"Have it your way." Vance banged twice on the side of the container. A few seconds later the door opened and he was passed a round object wrapped in plastic. He strode to the prisoner and emptied it into his lap.

Simeon screamed when he realized it was the head of his man Matra. Carved into Matra's forehead were three words.

UAE GET OUT

He bucked his hips and the head dropped off his lap and rolled across the floor. "What—what—what the fuck, you—you sick fucking animals!" he stuttered.

Vance chuckled. "Not much of a talker, is he?"

Simeon's eyes remained fixed on his former enforcer's mutilated forehead.

"As you can see, Mr. Isayev, I'm pretty serious about this message."

"I—I'll take it, I'll deliver your message."

"Where?"

"What do you mean?"

"Where will you take the message?"

"To my boss."

"Very good, and what's his name?"

Simeon was still staring at the head. "Karelin... Aslan Karelin."

"And where is Aslan?"

Simeon continued to stare at the bloodied head.

"My patience is wearing thin, Mr. Isayev. Where does Aslan live?"

"Limassol, Cyprus. I'll take the message to him in Cyprus. He has a house on the beach there."

"Good." Vance knelt down close to the man's face. His mouth was almost touching his ear. "You tell Aslan Karelin to get his business the fuck out of the UAE, or I'm going to come for him. Do you understand?"

Simeon's eyes never left the decapitated head of his man. "Yes, yes," he repeated, almost as if in a trance. "I will tell him." His face was deathly white.

Vance left him in the container. Once outside in the hangar he tore off his balaclava, pulled out his phone, and sent a text as he walked across to the planning room. Mitch, Ice, and Bishop were waiting for him.

"How did it go?" asked Bishop.

"Good, he sang like a canary. The carving on the head was a nice touch. Who was that?"

Both Bishop and Ice turned to Mitch. The Brit was wearing bloodstained coveralls.

"What? Bloody hell, guys, it's just a head. Don't tell me you get a bit squeamish at the first sign of blood?"

"Wouldn't have picked you for a psycho people butcher," said Vance.

"My old man was an undertaker, guys. Corpses stopped bothering me at age three."

"So what are we going to do with Simeon?" asked Ice.

"I texted this Aslan guy's details to Tariq. If it checks out we'll send Simeon on his way. If it doesn't Mitch might have to get a little more creative." He got up from his chair. "In the meantime I'm going to hit the gym."

———

"THAT THE INFO ON KARELIN?" Vance walked into the planning room with a gym towel draped over his broad shoulders and a protein shake in hand.

Bishop glanced up from the thick pile of documents he was flicking through. "Yep, one of Tariq's people dropped it off. I didn't want to interrupt your workout. Hope you don't mind, I took a look."

Vance collapsed into a chair as he drank from the shake. "Not at all, bud. Anything worthwhile?"

"Yeah, they've got a bit of dirt on Karelin. Simeon's telling the truth. He's the boss of one of the richest Russian mafia families. Spends most of his time at a beach-side villa in Cyprus; throws mega parties when he's on the island."

"Bit of a Hugh Hefner wannabe."

"Pretty much, this file's got the villa linked to drugs, prostitution, illegal gambling. When he's not at his beach house he's back in Russia."

"So where do you think he is now?"

"Considering it's winter in Mother Russia, my money's on him being in Cyprus. The villa is just outside Limassol."

"Makes sense." Vance finished off his shake. "Any photos?"

"Nope, and no description. Weird because it's not like he's maintaining a low profile. I reckon if we dropped into Cyprus we'd ID him pretty quick."

"I concur. Everything lines up with what Simeon is saying; might be time to turn our boy loose."

"Let him run to his master." Bishop nodded. The gangster was still tied to his chair in the shipping container.

The door to the room opened and Mitch walked in, still wearing bloodstained coveralls. "Lads, what's up?"

"We've got the police file on Aslan Karelin," said Vance. "And?"

"Looks like we're heading to Cyprus."

"So, you're going to cut our Russian friend loose?"

"Yep, you finished with his phone?"

"Sorted. If we get within a few hundred meters you can pick up the transmitter with this." Mitch reached into his pocket and placed an MP3 player on the table. "It will beep when it detects the signal. The faster it beeps, the closer it is to our man's phone."

"So you have to listen to it?" asked Bishop.

"No, you can set it to vibrate only."

"That's handy."

"Glad you approve because you'd better pack it," said Vance. "I'm sending you to Cyprus to find this guy's beach house."

"Too easy. And what about the rest of the team?"

"Once you've ID'd Karelin we'll be there. I think our message from Simeon will be more effective if we reinforce it with a little more finesse, and by finesse I mean firepower."

"Nice." Bishop smiled.

"Mitch, I need you to dump our friend here in the desert. Get Ice to help you." Vance got up from the table. "Not too far out. We do need him to get back to his boss."

"Can do. I'll let him keep the head for company." Mitch was already on his way out the door.

"So what's your plan going to be?" Vance asked once Mitch had left.

"The party scene has the best chance," Bishop said, thinking. "I'll probably need to hire a girl to make the connections; the file said the Karelin family runs all the high-class prostitution in Limassol."

"And your cover?"

"Typical Yank socialite. You know, lives large. Has a crack at gambling away daddy's trust fund."

"Right, I guess you're going to need some cash if we're going to pass you off as a rich American playboy."

Bishop grinned. "Sounds good to me."

"Tariq will have his people make all the arrangements.

Once you're ready, Mitch will fly you in on the business jet."
He got up, then stopped halfway to the door. "Everything
else OK, bud?"

"Yeah, I'm OK. Just taking it one day at a time."

"Ain't we all."

Chapter Fourteen

CYPRUS

BISHOP POURED himself a glass of champagne and sat back in the luxurious seats of the Rolls-Royce Phantom. The limousine, complete with black-capped chauffeur, had been waiting for him at the airport when he landed. He smiled as he lifted the glass to his lips. He was certainly dressed the part: cream-colored slacks, Italian leather boat shoes, a smart blue polo, and a sports jacket. He looked and felt every inch the wealthy American playboy that he was supposed to be.

Gazing out the window, he sipped from the glass, watching the countryside race by as the Phantom cruised on the A6 highway that joined Paphos with Limassol. The countryside reminded him of southern Spain. Outcrops of limestone on the low hills, dry scrubby vegetation, and plantations of olives and citrus interspaced between villages and towns. As his mind wandered, his thoughts turned to his parents. A ball of grief almost choked him and he fought to suppress his emotions, forcing his mind back to the present, to the mission that the others were relying on him to complete.

Bishop glanced at the platinum Omega Speedmaster on his wrist, another recent addition. It was ten in the morning; he had an entire day to fill before the nightclubs opened and the town started to party. Vance had only given him seventy-two hours to complete his mission to find the mafia boss. PRIMAL's leader wanted to maintain the pressure on the Russians, or, as he so eloquently put it, stamp on the turd while it was still steaming.

The limousine slowed as they entered the town of Limassol. Bishop had asked the driver to follow the coast road to the hotel, and they cruised past the lines of holiday apartments and condominiums. Lowering the window, he inhaled the fresh seaside air. It was obvious why the town was so popular with the expatriate Russian community. It lacked the glamor of the French Riviera or Amalfi Coast, but the climate was on par and the local property prices better value. More importantly for the Russian mafia, the foreign investment and banking laws were lax.

Near the end of the town the Phantom slowed and pulled up outside the lobby of the Le Méridien Spa and Resort. "Your hotel, sir."

"Thank you very much." Bishop dragged out his *r*'s slightly, turning his usually clipped Australian accent into a hint of an American drawl. He tipped the man and walked inside.

The lobby was fresh, with a nautical theme. Honey-colored wooden floors, polished marble benches and attractive staff wearing crisp white shirts. It reminded Bishop of a cruise ship.

"Hello." Bishop strolled up to the reception desk with a bellboy and his bespoke leather luggage in tow.

A beautiful receptionist with vibrant blue eyes looked up and flashed him a smile. "Hello sir, how can I help you?"

"My name is Anthony Newport." He placed his US passport and a credit card on the desk. "I have a reservation."

"Of course, Mr. Newport. We've been expecting you." She checked in his credit card and returned it along with the passport. "If you would follow me." Leaving her desk, she directed him toward one of the elevators. "We've got you in the Presidential Suite."

At the top floor she led him down a short corridor and opened the door to his suite. "Would you like me to show you around?" She gave a suggestive look.

"No, that's quite all right."

"Your luggage will be up in a moment."

She left with a smile and Bishop took the opportunity to explore the apartment. It was unlike anything he had ever stayed in. His wage as an Australian officer had been generous but this was way out of his league. He opened the sliding doors and strolled out onto a decked courtyard. The view from the private pool was stunning; it overlooked the hotel's grounds and out to the blue waters of the Mediterranean. "Holy shit!" he murmured under his breath. He did not want to know what this was costing Tariq each night. He smiled, the reality of working for an extremely well-resourced company was only just sinking in.

The doorbell snapped him out of his daze. He walked across and let the bellboy in.

"Is there anything else you need?" the young man asked as Bishop tipped him for delivering his bags.

"Matter of fact, there is. I'm new in town and I'd really

like someone to show me around." He smiled. "Preferably of the female variety, if you know what I mean."

"Of course, sir." The bellboy didn't miss a beat. "Perhaps there is a particular style of woman that you would like?"

"Well, now that you mention it, I've always been partial to Russians."

"Yes sir, very good sir."

"Highest quality of course, money's no issue." He handed over a few more crisp notes. "I'm going to be in town a few days and I'd love some company for the whole time."

The bellboy nodded. "I will have someone call you when she arrives. Perhaps you could meet her at the bar later this evening to see if you get along."

"That would be splendid. Gives me enough time to unpack and freshen up."

———

SEVEN HOURS later Bishop strolled into the Promenade Lounge on the ground floor. The bar was tastefully decorated in a similar manner to the reception area. Warm wooden floors, white ceilings and walls, and huge windows that looked out over the hotel grounds. Long white rayon curtains rippled in the cool ocean breeze.

Bishop sat at the black polished bar on a stool. He'd changed his slacks and polo for a dark-blue suit and white shirt, open at the collar. The sun had set and he thought the attire would be more suitable for a drink with a strange woman in a five-star hotel, even if she was of the 'working' class.

He spotted her as soon as she entered the room. Long

and slender legs drew the eye first, expensive-looking heels accented her calves. Her dress hugged every curve revealing an ample bust and lean stomach. Light-brown hair cascaded over her shoulders like a horse's mane. She strutted confidently across the room to where Bishop was sitting.

He stood as she came closer. Her facial features were exquisite: a thin nose, full lips, high cheekbones, and beautiful gray eyes. This was not at all what he was expecting. He offered his hand with a small amount of trepidation. "Hello, my name is Anthony."

"My name is Katya," she purred softly in her Russian accent. "It is a pleasure to meet you, Anthony."

"The pleasure is all mine. Can I order you a drink?"

They chatted at the bar for almost an hour as they swapped cover stories. Bishop's expectation of a trashy Russian escort was completely dispelled. Katya spoke flawless English and claimed an expensive education at an Ivy League college.

After a few of the hotel's most expensive cocktails Bishop asked her what they did for fun in Limassol. An arched eyebrow suggested something a little more intimate than he intended. "There's time for that later," he said smiling. "Are there any clubs?"

"Of course there are." Her eyes lit up. "I can get us into all the best clubs."

"Excellent, but how about we start the evening with a bite to eat?"

"That's a good idea, what do you feel like?"

"I've heard the seafood around here is very good."

"I know just the place."

"Bartender, can you have the car meet us around the front. We're going to hit the town."

———

BISHOP SAT on his balcony watching the soft glow of the sun rising over the Mediterranean. Since his parent's death, sleep had been difficult for him. Every time he closed his eyes he saw their faces, and feelings of guilt came flooding in. It took every ounce of his willpower to push the thoughts from his head and focus on the here and now.

The girl, Katya, had passed out still dressed on the king-size bed. They had danced until the early hours of the morning in no less than a dozen different night spots, most of them Russian owned. Bishop had thrown huge amounts of money around, buying overpriced bottles of champagne like they were soft drinks. He had regulated his own alcohol intake carefully, ensuring he only become mildly inebriated.

The pocket of his jacket began vibrating and he reached around to where it was hanging on his chair. He thought it might have been the MP3 player. He had carried Mitch's receiver since he arrived but it was silent. Sifting around the pockets he pulled out his cell phone. As he answered the call he slid the door to the bedroom closed. "Anthony speaking."

"Bish, it's Vance. Didn't wake you up, did I?"

"I was just watching the sunrise."

"With your lady friend?" Vance dropped a romantic note into his tone.

Bishop laughed. "Negative, she's currently passed out on the bed."

"Ah Russians, they love their booze."

"They certainly do. Plus six straight hours of dancing and only a salad for dinner, poor thing's exhausted."

"Yeah, I bet you've really worn her out."

Bishop shook his head smiling. "Now, you can't live

vicariously through me, Vance, and I'm pretty sure this isn't a welfare call. So what's up."

"You had any luck locating Simeon and the Mafia boss's Villa?"

"Not yet, I just got here. I'm not real keen to straight-up ask, but I'll try and get the girl to take me there tonight."

"That shouldn't be too much of a problem for a young stud like you."

"The problem is I'm going to run out of cash. People party bloody hard in this part of the world."

"Not likely, bud, we already wired you another two hundred K to your account."

"That should see me through another day or two."

"Have you got any info on Simeon's boss yet?" Vance asked.

"Negative, Karelin actually seems to lay pretty low, despite the parties and the hookers."

"That's why we need you inside."

"I'm on it."

"I want this op wrapped up in the next twenty-four hours, Bish. No rest for the wicked."

"OK, next twenty-four hours. Got it," said Bishop wearily. "I'll check in as soon as I have positive ID on Karelin."

"Roger, we're relocating to Beirut to pick up a boat. Gonna sail from there to your location. Getting weapons in Cyprus was going to be too much of a goatfuck. You'll be able to reach me on the satellite phone."

"OK, I'll check in tomorrow." Bishop dropped the phone back into his jacket and lay on a chaise lounge to watch the sunrise. In a matter of minutes his head had fallen back and he was finally asleep.

Chapter Fifteen

KARELIN VILLA, ZYGI, CYPRUS

ASLAN KARELIN STRETCHED out on a recliner next to the pool in front of his beachside villa. Clad only in a pair of red swimming trunks, he bore a passing resemblance to the *Star Wars* character Jabba the Hutt. Thick rolls of fat had overtanned into mottled flesh that rippled with his every move. There could not have been a woman on the planet who found the fifty-year-old attractive. Yet the loungers around him were festooned with long tanned legs, peroxide-blonde hair, and fake breasts. A smorgasbord of prostitutes and gold diggers at his beck and call, such was the power of being one of the island's most affluent residents.

The mafia boss was one of the most successful Russian criminals to emerge from the former Soviet Union. The twenty-bedroom villa behind him was evidence enough of that. His parties were renowned across the island for being the wildest and invitations were highly prized.

While most of the partygoers realized that the obese

Russian was a criminal, they had no idea he also ran a legitimate multinational enterprise spanning half a dozen countries. Having no concept of ethics and able to leverage muscle when required, his businesses rapidly consumed any opposition.

"Boss, Simeon is here," a burly guard said, waking Aslan from his slumber. The man had an AKS-74U carbine slung across his back.

"Good, send him over." Aslan sat up, wrapping his impressive girth in a robe. He spotted his lieutenant skirting the swimming pool. "Simeon, my boy, how are you?"

"I've been better, boss."

"Come, sit. Tell me about this problem."

It took Simeon a few minutes to outline the sequence of events that had led to him fleeing the UAE.

"So we know nothing of these people?" the Mafia boss asked once he was finished.

Simeon shook his head. "They appeared out of nowhere, destroyed my operation, then disappeared like fucking ghosts."

"Calm down, Simeon, you're acting like a scared girl."

"They dropped me in the desert with Matra's fucking head and you want me to calm down?"

"What do you mean 'Matra's head'?"

"What do you think I mean? They butchered Matra, chopped off his head, and gave it to me."

"Hmm, interesting." Aslan snapped his fingers and an attendant appeared. He ordered two drinks. "The man who interrogated you was an American?"

Simeon nodded. "He definitely had an American accent. I think he was a Negro, a big fucking Negro. He wanted me to bring you the message, the one I gave you on the phone."

The drinks arrived and Aslan handed one to his subordinate. "You said they want us to cease all activities in the Emirates."

Simeon took the drink and finished it with one gulp. "Yes, or they said they would come for you."

Aslan laughed. "They can fucking try."

"Boss, it might be wise for us to lay low over in Dubai for a while. Maybe look at increasing our footprint somewhere else while we find out who did this."

"That's not bad advice, Simeon." Aslan smiled. "But I have already put a plan in place to deal with this problem."

"And?"

"Tomorrow a team of specialists will arrive from Russia: eight of our best men, all ex-Spetsnaz. You will take them to the UAE, find our enemies, and kill them."

"I still don't think that's—"

"Enough!" Aslan ordered, jowls wobbling. "Prove to me that you are still worthy to be my lieutenant." He lifted himself off the lounger with a grunt and waddled toward the villa. "Use your time here to pull yourself together. Relax and enjoy the party tonight."

Simeon sat in a chair and studied one of the ridiculously expensive yachts sailing along the coast. The idea of going back to Dubai to face the men who had kidnapped him was terrifying. The way he looked at it, he had twenty-four hours to convince Aslan that he was more use here in Cyprus.

Chapter Sixteen

BEIRUT-RAFIC HARIRI INTERNATIONAL AIRPORT, LEBANON

THE GULFSTREAM TOUCHED down at Beirut's international airport at midday. Mitch taxied the aircraft off the end of the main runway and angled it toward a hangar. Lascar Logistics ran a freight service out of the facility and it would serve as PRIMAL's point of arrival.

"Very smooth, Mitch, nicely done," Vance said as he and Ice walked down the stairs from the aircraft carrying their backpacks.

Mitch followed them. "Thanks, old man, and to think I've only ever flown it in a simulator."

"What the hell?" said Vance. "You kidding me?"

"Why would I be kidding?" Mitch said with a wink.

A Lascar Logistics employee and a Beirut customs official met them at the bottom of the stairs. "Welcome to Beirut, gentlemen," said the Lascar man as the government official inspected their passports. "Your vehicle is outside," he added, handing Vance the keys.

"Thanks."

"How long will you be staying?" the official asked as he handed back the passports. A number of well-placed bribes had ensured the team's entry into the country with only the most token of formalities.

"Just a few days," said Vance. "Our boss has arranged a boat for us to cruise around the Med."

"Ah, very nice. Well, everything is in order here. Enjoy your stay."

A Lascar contractor had already unloaded the aircraft and they grabbed their kit bags, heading out of the hangar and through an airport security checkpoint. A van was parked on the other side.

"I think you're the only one who knows where we're going, Mitch." Vance threw him the keys.

Mitch drove them along the coast road, heading north. They passed endless apartment blocks on the foreshore, many under construction as the city continued to rebuild following the civil war of the eighties.

"They've come a long way since I was last here," said Vance.

"When was that? Mid-nineties with Charlie Sheen?" joked Ice.

"Christ, that was a bad movie." Vance laughed.

"Because it was about SEALs. No one ever made a bad movie about Marines."

"That's because they're angry muthas. No one likes to piss off a Marine; they'll go all Lee Harvey Oswald on your ass."

The banter continued for twenty minutes before they

arrived at the marina, parking next to the office. The door jingled as Mitch led them in. The man behind the counter was portly, with a caterpillar-like mustache lodged above his infectious smile.

"You should have a boat ready for a Mr. Braithwaite," Mitch said in his crisp accent.

"Ah yes, the *Princessa Bella*, a very fine craft." He checked his paperwork. "Everything has been taken care of already. If you would follow me, please."

The *Princessa Bella* was a Sea Ray 560, fifty-six feet of sleek lines, chromed railings, and powerful engines. She was capable of cruising at a comfortable thirty knots and had more than enough range for their needs.

"She'll do just nicely," said Vance as they stowed their bags below.

"I'll leave you chaps to sort things out." Mitch turned to leave. "I've got to catch up with an old friend."

"You sure you don't want to take Ice with you?"

"No mate, I'll be alright. This is Beirut, not Glasgow."

———

IT TOOK Mitch ten minutes to drive from the marina to Beirut's main shipping port. He pulled into one of the container terminals and stopped in front of a boom gate. "I'm here to see Mr. Azooz," he told the guard.

"OK, OK. Down there on the left." The guard raised the boom and indicated with a wave of his hand.

Driving between the towering stacks of cargo containers, he slowed as a huge crane swung a container out over the pathway. He waited until it was clear before continuing to a warehouse. Parking the van out the front, he strolled into a workshop where two men were working on a dilapidated forklift.

"You need a hand there, gents?"

"Mr. Mitch, I would know that beautiful voice anywhere." The man pulled his head out from under the forklift and wiped his greasy hands clean on ragged coveralls.

"It's good to see you, Azooz. Been a long time," Mitch said as they shook hands.

"It has, oh it has. I was so excited to receive your order. I did not expect that you would be picking it up personally. Will you be in town for long?"

"No, old man, just a few hours. I'm actually in a bit of a hurry."

"No problems at all, your shipment is complete." He led the way through the warehouse and out the back through a doorway.

The area behind the workshop was occupied by a row of containers.

"Some of the things you asked for were very hard to find. I'm afraid it's going to be a little more expensive than I originally quoted you."

"How much more?" asked Mitch.

"Forty thousand."

"Sounds like you're trying to stiff me, Azooz."

"No, Mr. Mitch, things have changed. Western guns are harder to get now. Lots of my old friends have gone out of business. The market is flooded with all of the cheap stuff coming out of Russia. You know, the Curtain comes down and they flood the market with junk."

They stopped at a container and Azooz unlocked it, cracked the doors, and invited Mitch inside.

"You first, Azooz."

The inside of the container smelled dry and dusty. It was empty except for a stack of boxes covered by an oil-stained plastic sheet.

"Ta-da!" Azooz pulled back the cover to reveal a MAG58 machine gun and a Barrett Light 50 sniper rifle.

"Very nice, Azooz, you've outdone yourself." Mitch inspected the two weapons; they were almost brand-new.

"I told you, I always have the best. There is special ammunition and also this." He took a small plastic case from the top of a pile of ammunition boxes and opened it. Inside was a device that looked like a laser pointer.

"Well done, old man." Mitch inspected the gadget. "This will do the job nicely. What about the tripod for the Gimpy, and the other gear?"

"Yes, it is all here." He pulled back the sheet further, revealing the tripod for the machine gun and a duffel bag. "I put the pistols inside as well."

Mitch unzipped the bag and checked the contents. "I'll need to borrow a few tools."

"No problems, you can use anything in the workshop." Azooz stood next to Mitch for a few seconds then gave a cough.

"Oh yeah," said Mitch. "Suppose you'd be wanting cash." He reached into his jacket and took out an envelope. "Here's the originally agreed price."

"But..." Azooz feigned shock.

"Keep your alans on, mate. Here's another fifty K for your efforts. The people I work for appreciate good service."

"Ah, thank you, Mr. Mitch. My men will load your van while you work."

It took Mitch twenty minutes to fabricate what he needed using the parts Azooz had supplied. By then the Lebanese merchant's men had loaded all the weapons into the van and he left with a wave. Another fifteen minutes and he pulled up next to the wharf alongside the *Princessa Bella*.

"You got everything we need?" Vance yelled down from the bridge. He'd managed to acquire a Captain's hat and was wearing it at a jaunty angle.

"All good, skipper."

"Let's load up, cast off, and get this show on the road."

————

LE MERIDIEN SPA AND RESORT, LIMASSOL

"What do you want to do tonight, Tony?" Katya purred from where she was sprawled across the king-size bed in her underwear.

Bishop was in the bathroom, relaxing in the oversize bathtub, a glass of champagne in his hand. "I thought we could do something a little more exciting than clubs. Is there a casino in this town?"

Katya rolled over onto her elbows, revealing devastating cleavage for her slim frame. "No, you silly man, there is no casino in Limassol. Gambling is outlawed. We can go to Turkey, they have casinos there."

"A little far to go for a night out, don't you think? Surely there's something a little closer."

"I might know of something."

"An underground casino?" Bishop sat up in the bath. "I've heard of such things. Do you know of any?"

She laughed. "Not so much a casino as a wild party. A friend of mine has a place up the coast. I've got to warn you though, they're pretty crazy and it could cost you a lot of cash."

Bishop grinned like a Cheshire cat. "Sweetheart, if there's one thing I've got it's plenty of cash."

"Then it shouldn't be a problem. Now how about you get out of that bath and come and pay some attention to me."

"No, how about you come and get in this bath and pay me some attention."

Chapter Seventeen

KARELIN VILLA

IT HAD TAKEN Bishop and Katya thirty minutes to reach the villa from Limassol. The Rolls-Royce had followed the winding coast road east before reaching a small town called Zygi; at least that's what Bishop thought the faded signpost said. A short trip down a dirt road had put them on a remote stretch of coastline, the shimmering Mediterranean sea visible under the moonlit night. The only lights in the area were coming from the villa complex; it was the perfect location for someone wanting privacy.

Pounding bass penetrated the cabin as the limousine pulled up to the well-lit security gates. A thick rendered wall, topped with razor wire, surrounded the opulent palace.

Katya lowered her window and spoke, in Russian, to the two guards manning the gate. They were serious-looking thugs with the obligatory bulge of a sidearm under their suit jackets. One of them checked the car thoroughly, searching the trunk and the underside.

"Very exciting," whispered Bishop. "Just like a Bond movie." He spotted an AK leaning against the wall in the guard box.

Katya gave him a smile. "Yes, darling. Just like a Bond movie."

As they drove through the gates and onto the villa grounds the MP3 player in Bishop's jacket vibrated once. Simeon, or at least his phone, was close by.

"Wow!" Bishop took in the sheer extravagance of the floodlit residence. It sported two sandstone staircases that curved up from the driveway and met at the landing. Tall marble columns held up a red tile–capped roof that covered no less than four huge balconies. The estate could have belonged in ancient history, perched among olive groves on the hills overlooking Rome. However, instead of chariots and white-robed nobles, the estate featured sports cars and scantily clad hookers.

He gave Katya a broad smile. "I think we are going to have a lot of fun tonight."

She grabbed him by the front of his shirt and kissed him. "Yes, we are."

They pulled up at the stairs and the chauffeur opened the door. Katya stepped out into the warm night air in another of her figure-hugging dresses.

"That will be all, James," Bishop said to the driver, turning on his best British accent.

Katya giggled and pulled him up the stairs.

"In all seriousness, I don't think I'm going to need you again tonight," said Bishop over his shoulder.

"Very good, sir. You have my number." The Rolls drove past a long line of guests' cars and out an automatic gate.

Bishop and Katya climbed the stairs hand in hand, drawing more than a few glances from the other guests.

"Who is this guy?" A Russian with a jagged scar running down one cheek prodded Bishop with a metal-detecting wand.

"He's a friend of mine," said Katya, hanging off Bishop's arm. "A very wealthy friend of mine," she added in Russian.

"I don't care," said the guard. "No one gets in without Karelin's approval, no one."

"What's going on here?"

Bishop recognized the voice immediately. The constant vibration of the MP3 player in his jacket confirmed it.

Simeon Isayev appeared in the mansion's doorway dressed in a business suit. He had a martini glass in one hand and wore a scowl on his face. He made eye contact with Bishop and stared at him for a few seconds. "Do I know you?"

"I don't think so." Bishop thrust out his hand. "Name's Anthony Newport."

The Russian continued to study his face as he shook his hand. "I'm sure I know you."

"No sir, I doubt that," Bishop continued. "Not unless you spend a lot of time in Oregon or you're in the fertilizer business."

"No." Simeon shook his head. "Never mind." He turned to Katya. "What seems to be the problem, my dear?"

"This big oaf doesn't want to let Mr. Newport in." She left Bishop's side and grasped the Mafia lieutenant's shoulder as she whispered in his ear. "He has a lot of money and nowhere to gamble with it."

Simeon smiled. "Any friend of Katya is a friend of

mine," he declared, waving them past the guards and into the hedonistic house of the Karelin Russian Mafia. "Come, Mr. Newport, we should find you a drink."

"That sounds like a fantastic idea." Bishop reached into his jacket and deactivated the MP3 player. Its mission was complete.

"You go on ahead," said Katya. "I'm going to get changed into my swimsuit."

Simeon led Bishop through the ground floor of the mansion, past mingling guests, and out to the entertaining area at the back. "What do you drink, Mr. Newport?" he asked over the electro music banging from the speakers that had been set up around the pool.

"Please, call me Tony. I'll have a vodka on the rocks with a twist of lemon."

While Simeon ordered drinks Bishop surveyed the scene. The villa was equally impressive at the rear; folding windows, or maybe they were doors, meant that the living space on the bottom floor blended seamlessly with the outdoor patio. It ran straight into a long pool filled with scantily clad women. On the other side of the pool there was twenty yards or so of grass before the white sands of the beach and the waters of the Mediterranean.

The entire setting was strewn with glamorous women and wealthy men, an age-old stereotype reinforced by an endless supply of drugs, alcohol, and cash. There was a DJ at the end of the bar working his decks and enjoying the attention of at least a dozen dancing floozies. Colored lights above the DJ booth seemed to flash in time with the heavy bass line. Out to sea a flotilla of expensive-looking boats were anchored, the lights reflecting off the glass and chrome fixtures. Bishop had to admit it was an epic party.

"So, Tony," Simeon handed him a drink. "What brings you to Cyprus, business or pleasure?"

"Well, I had just finished meetings in Africa. Thought I'd drop by your island for some fun."

"First time here?"

"Yeah, wanted to check it out. Heard you Russians knew how to party."

"Ah, and I trust that Katya has been a good host?"

"Oh yes, she's amazing."

"That she is." Simeon took a drink from his glass. "You mentioned fertilizer, is that a very lucrative industry in America?"

"Very, my father owns the company. It makes well over fifty million in profit annually."

"You work for your father?"

"Yes, unfortunately, I'm his run-around guy. I get sent to every shithole in the world to meet with his clients and keep them happy."

"Then we have something in common." He lifted his glass. "To shitholes and ungrateful bosses."

Bishop raised his glass. "To shitholes and ungrateful bosses!"

As they drank Katya appeared from inside the villa. She had changed into a sleek white single-piece swimsuit that left very little to the imagination. She strode across to the pool and used the stairs to lower herself slowly into the water.

Bishop's eyes followed her and Simeon smiled. "Tell me Tony, do you play poker?"

"Yes, I do." He continued to watch Katya as she swum gracefully across the pool.

"Some of us are about to play upstairs; there's room for

one more." Simeon took a cigar from his jacket and offered it to him. "Perhaps you would join us."

Bishop took the cigar. "I would be honored."

"The game will go late, but we have plenty of spare rooms that you and Katya can enjoy."

"This night just keeps getting better."

Simeon laughed. "We'll see how happy you are by morning when I've taken all your money."

"We'll see. I'm not half-bad at Texas Hold'em."

———

PRINCESSA BELLA, MEDITERRANEAN SEA

The engines of the cruiser throbbed as she sliced gracefully through the calm waters of the Mediterranean. Vance was at the helm, his captain's cap insulating his bald head from the cool night air. They had been underway for a little over five hours and the sun had just slipped below the horizon. Time at the helm had initially been shared between the three of them but now that it was dark the other two men had gone below to prepare their equipment.

Mitch was at work in the master bedroom converting the bag filled with detonators, batteries, firing circuits, and cell phones into two remote-activated gunfire simulators. Once he had finished soldering the wiring he wrapped the two devices in plastic and tape, and stowed them back in the bag. Then he moved into the galley, where Ice was working.

"How's the skipper doing?" Mitch asked.

"Good, I just took him up a coffee. We're about ten minutes away from dropping anchor and getting some sleep." Ice had both the sniper rifle and the machine gun set up on the dining table. He'd used rubber caps on their bipods to stop them slipping on the laminated surface.

"Yeah, a bit of rack time wouldn't go astray. How are our guns looking?"

"The MAG's good to go, gave her a clean. The fifty's a different matter. I'm not confident I'm going to be able to put a decent zero on her."

"I've got something for that." Mitch opened one of the kitchen lockers and pulled out a black plastic case. He unclipped it, rummaged around, and pulled out a small black laser pointer and what looked like a spent .50 caliber casing. "What range you working with?" he asked as he screwed the laser into the casing.

"If we zero 1.5 inches at one hundred yards we should be on the money."

"Chamber this." Mitch passed the round to Ice, who pulled back the bolt, dropped it into the breech, and closed it again.

"This will give us a pretty close zero." Mitch took out a piece of paper and ducked back into the master bedroom, where he taped the target to the front bulkhead. "If you aim at the bull's-eye the dot should be about one point low."

Ice aimed the big rifle through the doorway, lining his sights up on the target. The laser in the casing shone down the barrel, superimposing on the sniper scope's reticle. "On the money out of the box. Your man's pretty efficient, bro."

"I only work with the best." Mitch grinned. "Let's knock up a few targets and put a few rounds downrange."

They inflated six balloons, half-filling them with water and a cracked glow stick before they took the two weapons and ammunition above deck.

"Vance, are we right to test-fire these guns?" Mitch asked as Ice set up the weapons at the back of the boat.

"Not a problem, bud." Vance pointed to the navigation screen. "We're about fifty nautical miles from Limassol and the radar's all clear."

Mitch gave a thumbs-up and began dumping glowing balloons overboard.

Ice pulled his hearing protection on and settled into a seated firing position on one of the swivel chairs at the stern. The heavy sniper rifle rested on a fiberglass table. He watched the glowing orb grow smaller as they left it behind and when it reached about a hundred meters he yelled out, "Ears!"

The other men placed their fingers in their ears.

The .50-cal belched flame and the glowing balloon disappeared. "Smack on," said Ice. He sighted another balloon and repeated the process at two hundred, three hundred, and four hundred meters.

"She's pretty good." He set the sniper rifle down on the deck and replaced it with the machine gun. He loaded up a fifty-round belt and actioned the gun. "You want to have a go?" he asked Mitch.

"Sure, why not." The burly technician sat behind the machine gun and tucked it into his shoulder.

Ice dropped the two last balloons over the back. Mitch waited until the targets reached a hundred meters, thumbed off the safety, and squeezed the trigger.

The gun shuddered, climbing upward as it spat rounds. Three full-metal-jacket bullets disappeared into the darkness before a tracer round shot skyward, a green streak arcing away from the boat.

Mitch adjusted his position and hammered out another burst. This time the rounds arced out toward the balloons and one of them disappeared.

"Hit!" Ice said. "Now the last one."

The final balloon was rapidly shrinking, barely visible in the darkness. Mitch let off another burst. He missed. Two more bursts followed, the last one sending the target to the bottom.

"Solid drills," said Ice. "Good to know we've got another gunner if we need it."

Vance throttled back the engines as the two men joined him on the bridge. "We've got about another two hours before we hit Limassol."

"You heard anything from Bish?" Ice asked as he studied the nautical map on the GPS screen.

"Negative, no calls. If he doesn't make contact in the next ten minutes we'll anchor up and wait 'til tomorrow."

"I'll head below and make us some more coffee," said Mitch as he disappeared down the stairs.

"Bishop sound OK when you last spoke to him?" asked Ice.

"Yeah bud, why?"

"I just get the feeling he's got a lot bottled up inside."

"We all do. I don't think you can be in this business without being a little broken. You don't have a problem with him, do you?"

"Not at all, he's a good operator. I was just wondering, that's all."

"He's been through some serious shit recently, but he'll be fine. You just keep him out of trouble."

"Bit hard when you've got him gallivanting all over Cyprus with hookers and wads of cash."

Vance laughed. "You know what I mean."

Ice gazed out the window at a distant flashing green light. "Don't worry about it. I've got his back."

KARELIN VILLA

Bishop staggered into an empty bedroom and collapsed on the bed. He lay on his back and lifted his arm so he could read the luminous hands on his watch. It was three in the morning. He groaned and sat up feeling inside his jacket for his phone. The card game had destroyed him. It had started well but the Russians had insisted that they slam shots every time an ace appeared in the winning hand. He was amazed at how many times that occurred in the course of a game. They had finally called it quits when one of the other players had passed out at the table. Good thing, because Bishop was not far behind.

He sat up in bed and struggled to focus on the luminous blue buttons of his cell phone's keypad. Eventually he navigated the menus and dialed Vance's satellite phone.

Vance picked up on the second ring. "Bish, how's it going?"

"Not great."

"Buddy, you sound like you're smashed."

"Fucking Russians made me drink vodka."

Vance laughed. "So I take it you've found the villa?"

"Fuck yeah, I'm Shimeoinsh's new best friend. I even met that fat fuck Karelin. He plays cards like a girl."

"Look, we're about an hour or so from Limassol. If you can give us a description we'll find the place."

"Limassol? It's not in Limassol, it's in Ziggy."

"Ziggy? Do you mean Zygi, the town immediately to the east?"

"That's it. You can't miss it. It's got more lights on than anywhere else. Big swimming pool, lots of girls. Boats out the front. You know, it was an awesome party!" Bishop was getting animated.

"Thanks, buddy. That'll probably do it."

"No problem. Oh, and Vance."

"Yeah, buddy."

"I love you."

"Get some sleep, bud. I'll talk to you in the morning."

Bishop managed to drop the phone into his jacket before he passed out.

———

PRINCESSA BELLA

"That it?" Ice pointed at a villa glowing in the darkness. The two-story monstrosity was about six hundred yards away and lit up like a Christmas tree. There was a small fleet of luxury cruisers and yachts anchored offshore.

"Haven't seen anything else that gets even close to what Bishop described," said Vance as he checked the navigation system. "The GPS has us just off Zygi." He throttled back the engines.

"Looks like someone had a hell of a party." Mitch scanned with a pair of binoculars. "There's people passed out on those boats, and the beach." He scanned up to the mansion. A few bedrooms still had their lights on, silhouettes suggesting some of the guests were still continuing their partying in more private settings. "Blimey! There's some action going on in the bedrooms. I wonder if Bishop's still up."

"Not likely, he sounded like he was definitely ready for bed." Vance killed the motor cruiser's engines. "Ice, is this close enough?"

"This is fine." The former Marine was wearing a pair of reef walkers, black boardshorts decorated with a flower imprint, and a black neoprene vest. He climbed down from the bridge to the stern of the boat where he had laid his gear out on the table.

There was a clatter then a splash from the bow as Vance dropped the anchor.

"These good to go?" asked Ice as he picked up one of Mitch's distraction devices.

"Yeah mate, you just need to unwrap the plastic and find somewhere to hide them. Don't bury them, it'll muffle the sound."

"Got it." He packed the homemade explosives into a black dry bag along with an equipment belt containing a HK pistol, suppressor, and a short-range UHF radio. "Vance, I'll be at least an hour. If we lose comms and I'm not back by 0530, you might want to consider moving the boat west."

Vance gave him a thumbs-up from the bridge.

He slung the dry bag across his back and climbed down into the cool black water. He shivered, not from the cold but from the trepidation of entering the dark water. No matter how many times he did it, he still got that nervous jolt as his senses announced their disapproval of entering an environment where they were next to useless.

He set off toward the beach using breaststrokes to power through the small waves, aiming slightly to the left of the mansion and the other boats. The last thing he wanted was to run into any late-night skinny-dippers as he came in through the shallows.

Ice had swum for both his high school and college teams before joining the Marines. A former recon operator, he was a formidable swimmer and covered the distance to the shoreline in a few minutes.

As he waded ashore he could feel the sharp rock under the rubber of his shoes. He hunched low in the water, well outside the range of the mansion's lights. When the rocks underfoot gave way to sand, he slid forward and rode the waves into the beach. Then he dashed out of the water and crouched in the scrubby vegetation.

Opening his dry bag he retrieved the equipment belt. Once he checked the pistol was ready and secured on his hip he waited quietly in the darkness, watching for anything that might suggest compromise. Sensing nothing out of the ordinary he pulled the radio from the belt. "Can you hear me, Bella?" he transmitted quietly.

"Loud and clear, Beachcomber, have fun searching for buried treasure."

Ice placed the radio back in its pouch and worked his way inland from the beach, cautious for any sign of guards or security sensors. The estate had a six-foot chain fence at the very edge of the grounds. Black material blocked anyone from seeing inside. He moved along it until it reached a tall white wall. There was no sign of CCTV cameras or external lighting.

He retraced his steps until he found a spot where the black material had been torn from the fence by the wind. There was a hollow under the bottom of the wire that he could scrape clear and probably squeeze through if he needed to get inside.

He hid the first of Mitch's devices under a bush near the tear in the fence. The other he placed closer to the beach. With that done, he pulled out the radio. "Bella, this is Beachcomber. The pickings are slim here so I'm coming back."

"Sit tight, Comber, there's a nasty rip here."

Something was wrong. "OK, Bella, let me know when it's all clear." Ice settled into the line of bushes next to the beach and made himself comfortable. He checked his watch; there was about half an hour of darkness left. If Vance did not give him the all-clear soon it would be light and he would be stuck ashore.

Chapter Eighteen

KARELIN VILLA

"HEY, WAKE THE FUCK UP."

Bishop opened his eyes, blinking. When the blurriness cleared he realized he was staring into the scarred face of the angry security guard from the night before. "What do you want?" He sat up, noticing that Katya was not in the room.

"My boss wants to have a chat with you."

"Sure, no problems," Bishop mumbled looking around for a glass of water. "Just let me get cleaned up."

"No, he wants to talk to you now!"

Bishop checked his watch. "Look, man, it's eight o'clock. Let him know that I can make eight thirty. That's if he supplies the coffee."

"Get the fuck up!" The menace in the man's voice motivated Bishop to swing his legs over the side of the bed and stagger to his feet. He was still dressed in his clothes from last night, shoes included.

"Where's Simeon?" asked Bishop as he was led down-stairs and out onto the patio at the front of the villa. He squinted in the bright sunlight, head pounding. The vodka had left him feeling absolutely shattered.

Scarface ignored his questions and shoved him forward, past the swimming pool out onto the grass in front. The sunlight was reflecting off the ocean and Bishop felt like it was penetrating all the way to his brain.

On the grass a grossly overweight human being was sunning himself on a recliner. It was the same guy he had played cards with last night, Aslan, the boss. Bishop let out a breath as he tried not to vomit in his mouth. A quick glance around identified no less than six armed bodyguards, a couple with assault rifles.

"Good morning, Anthony." Simeon was sitting on a chair under an umbrella a short distance away. He was sipping from a tall glass of water.

"Simeon, what's this all about?"

"I was hoping you could tell me."

Bishop shook his head. "I don't understand. Look, if this is about the money I lost last night, it's all good. I can go to the hotel and get it right now."

"You're good, very good." Simeon smiled. "I don't think you even realize the game is up."

"Seriously, buddy, I'm in the dark here."

"Katya heard your phone call last night. She heard you tell someone that you found us. She heard you give someone directions here."

"I rang someone last night?" He reached into his jacket for his phone. It was missing.

"Looking for this?" Simeon was holding the cell phone. "This morning at four fifty you rang a number based in the USA."

"Oh, I remember, I rang my father." Bishop was immediately grateful that Tariq's people had the foresight to route calls to Vance's satellite phone through the US.

"Your father?" Simeon raised his eyebrows. "You called your father?"

"Yes, he likes me to check in. Otherwise he cuts off my funding." Bishop could see that Simeon was far from convinced. He was staring at the phone.

"Call him if you want. Ask him yourself," Bishop continued and poured himself a large glass of water from the table next to Simeon. The scarred security guard shadowed him, unsure whether to intervene.

"I might just do that."

Bishop gulped the water down.

"Simeon! Have you sorted this mess out yet?" Aslan yelled in Russian.

"I'm sorting it out now."

"Bring the fucking spy over here." Aslan sat up in the lounger and signaled for a robe.

"I hope you're telling the truth, for your sake." Simeon gave Scarface a nod and Bishop was shoved over to Aslan.

"So what the fuck is going on?" Aslan asked in Russian.

Simeon gave him a rundown on the situation.

"So what are you waiting for? Call the number, find out if this piece of shit is lying or just another dumbass American who owes me money."

Simeon nodded and hit redial on the phone.

———

PRINCESSA BELLA

"Vance, this doesn't look good, old man." Mitch was sitting at the rear of the *Bella*'s upper deck with the .50-caliber sniper rifle in his shoulder. He had cut a hole in the plastic weather shield to let the muzzle poke through. "They've got Bishop and they don't look happy. There's at least six guards." Through the scope he was watching Bishop being questioned by Simeon while a morbidly obese man watched from a chaise lounge.

"Motherfuckers. How the hell was he compromised?" Vance was observing through the binoculars. They had been monitoring the beach since the Russians had started patrolling it, ready to provide support if Ice or Bishop had to extract. That was almost four hours ago.

The satellite phone started ringing from where it was wedged in the boat's console. Vance picked it up and glanced at the screen. "It's Bishop's phone."

"Simeon's holding it," Mitch confirmed.

"You good to take a shot?"

"Who? The fatty on the chaise or Simeon?"

"The fat guy, that's got to be Aslan. Give Ice a heads-up." He threw the radio onto the deck next to Mitch as he answered the call.

"Hello?"

There was silence from the other end.

"Anthony, is that you?"

Still silence.

"Goddamn phone must be on the fritz," said Vance.

Mitch continued to monitor the scene at the villa through the scope of the sniper rifle as he whispered into the radio. He quickly brought Ice up to speed on the situation.

"Why do I know this voice?" Simeon's guttural accent came through accusingly.

"Who is this?" said Vance. "Put Tony on the phone."

There was a long pause.

Mitch lined up the crosshairs on Karelin, who was now sitting up. "This is going to be like shooting a pig at a feeding trough," he murmured.

Simeon continued, speaking softly, "It's you! The one from Dubai, I'd never forget that voice."

"I told you to tell your boss to get the fuck out. I told you I'd find you," Vance growled.

Mitch took up the slack in the trigger and breathed out.

The Russian's voice became more confident. "I told him, but he doesn't scare easily. You might have found us, but now we've got your man and he's going to tell us everything he knows. Maybe when I'm done you can have his fucking head back."

"Well, let's just hope you make better decisions than he does." Vance hung up. "Do it."

Mitch squeezed the trigger and the rifle belched flame.

Chapter Nineteen

KARELIN VILLA

MITCH'S ROUND hit the Russian Mafia boss square in the chest. The kinetic energy blew his grossly overweight body clean off the lounger, flipping him backward into the swimming pool where he bobbed like a harpooned whale in a spreading cloud of pink water.

"SNIPER!" screamed Scarface as he drew his pistol.

Simeon dove behind the outdoor bar as the gunmen with assault rifles returned fire in the direction of the motor cruiser anchored on the horizon.

Mitch kept firing the semiautomatic sniper rifle, emptying the ten-round magazine into the guards, the .50-caliber rounds sending limbs flying and splintering through palm trees.

More gunmen streamed out from the villa with assault rifles. Women that had been dozing by the pool screamed hysterically and hid behind whatever cover they could find.

"The boat! Shoot the boat!" yelled Simeon in Russian from his hiding place.

AKs clattered and rounds danced across the ocean, sending plumes of froth jetting into the air around the yachts anchored off the beach. Panicked guards blasted the closer boats as they attempted to hit the PRIMAL vessel farther offshore.

On the *Princessa Bella* Vance had hauled anchor and had them surging away from the coast. Mitch had managed to get off another ten-round magazine before it became too difficult to hold a sight picture as the bow crashed through the sea at full throttle. He stowed the .50 cal away and used his phone to activate the remote devices Ice had placed.

Gunshots exploded from the fence line to the west of the villa.

"We're under attack!" screamed Simeon. He had pulled a pistol from his pants and fired it randomly in the direction of the shots.

Bishop had already used the total confusion to make his escape. He'd sprinted across the lawn, skirted the pool and its screaming women, and dashed into the bottom level of the mansion. A few guards ran past carrying assault rifles, unaware he was a threat.

Back out on the lawn the Russians were still firing at the yachts and the fence line, even after the gunfire simulators had expired.

"Hold your fire!" Simeon scrambled to his feet. "Hold your fire!" He looked around for Anthony. "FIND THE FUCKING AMERICAN!"

Bishop was making a beeline for the front entrance and seeing two guards there he charged up a staircase.

Sprinting into the corridor he collided with Katya, bowling over the slender escort.

He stopped and helped her up. "Sorry to love you and leave you, babe," he quipped as he searched for another way out.

"STOP!" a voice behind him screamed.

Bishop dove into the closest room, slamming the door shut behind him, fumbling the lock closed. He nearly jumped out of his skin as a woman screamed. The prostitute was sitting bolt upright in bed, a client passed out next to her. Huge fake breasts wobbled as she continued her ear-splitting screech.

"Shut up!" Bishop screwed up his face as he pulled back the curtains to reveal one of the balconies that faced out from the front of the estate toward the road. Someone bashed on the door behind him.

"I hope you don't mind." Bishop grabbed some car keys from the bedside table and ran out to the balcony. Behind him the lock gave way and one of the Russian gangsters crashed into the room. Bishop climbed over the balcony, lowered himself down, and dropped with a thud onto the front landing of the mansion. When he leaped to his feet he was staring into the muzzles of two short-barreled AKs.

"Hi, guys." He stood slowly, raising his hands above his head.

"DOWN!" The voice came from behind.

He dropped to a knee and registered the snap of subsonic rounds as they zipped over his head. Two guards collapsed, their automatic weapons clattering on the marble. He spun to see Ice dressed in his flower-patterned board-shorts and black top, holding his suppressed HK.

"Nice outfit. How's the break?"

"Dead flat, bro. We've got to get out of here." Ice picked up one of the AKS-74Us the dead guards had dropped and holstered his pistol.

"Follow me." Bishop grabbed the other AK and they sprinted down the stairs toward the guests' cars.

Above them a weapon barked and bullets sparked off the sandstone. Ice spun and fired instinctively. His rounds sent the shooter on the balcony scurrying for cover.

Bishop ran along the line of exotic sports cars and limousines parked on the gravel frantically depressing the unlock button on the car keys. Lights flashed on a car toward the front of the line. "Bingo, we've got a ride."

"Maybe I should drive," said Ice as they ran to the car. "You smell like a distillery."

"Do you really want me manning the guns?" Bishop said as he pulled open the driver's door.

"Good point." Ice stopped as he reached for his door handle. "You've got to be shitting me. A Prius."

"Just shut up and get in." The hybrid car gave a whine as Bishop pressed the ignition button.

"Yeah, great, we'll really be able to outrun them in this," Ice grumbled to himself as he leaped into the backseat.

At that moment a pair of black Mercedes sedans sped through the gates and into the compound. They skidded to a halt in front of the stairs as the Prius raced past them toward the entrance.

"THE GATE! FUCKING SHUT THE GATE!" Simeon screamed from the front landing. He ran down the steps and pulled open the door to the first Mercedes. "Stay in the fucking car! Those guys, they killed Aslan." He pointed at the little Prius rocketing out of the estate, escaping from the villa as the gates closed behind it.

"Get after them and fucking kill them, fifty grand for their heads."

Karelin's Spetsnaz team reacted like a well-oiled machine. The driver of the lead vehicle turned the big car and gunned the engine, flicking the powerful sedan around on the gravel. He slammed his fist on the horn, prompting the guards to reopen the gates. Then he unleashed the power of the Mercedes's V8, hammering down the dirt road trailing a cloud of dust. "Two men in a hybrid," he said chuckling. "This will be the easiest fifty grand we ever made."

"Like shooting Chechens in a mosque," said one of the killers in the backseat as he cocked a submachine gun and wound down the window.

Behind them the second Mercedes barreled out of the gates and joined the chase.

Chapter Twenty

ZYGI, CYPRUS

"HEY, LOOK AT THE UPSIDE," said Bishop as he rallied the little hatchback along the coast toward Limassol. "If it comes to a long-distance race we're going to get fifty miles to the gallon."

"Always looking on the bright side, aren't you," Ice said from the backseat.

"I find it makes for a much more enjoyable journey through life," said Bishop as checked the rearview mirror. He had the accelerator pressed to the floor and the tiny engine was screaming like an enraged piglet.

Ice lowered his window. "I'll try Vance again." He angled the little UHF radio out toward the ocean.

"Bella, can you hear me? Bella, this is Comber, do you copy?" Ice put the radio back in his belt pouch. "Nothing, bro, we're on our own."

"Not exactly." Bishop could see one of the black sedans

in the rearview mirror. It was gaining fast. "I count one, no two, on our tail."

Ice glanced back. "If we don't shake these guys we're in real trouble." He checked the magazine on his AK; it was half-full. He did the same with Bishop's weapon which felt like it was full.

The coast road was winding and narrow, and the Prius with its superior economy offered zero advantage. The high-powered sedans were rapidly closing in.

Ice reached behind the headrests on the backseat and pulled up on the release. He wrenched one of the seat backs down. "Bish, the trunk release is down by your right foot."

"Please don't tell me you own a Prius."

"No, my sister does."

"I've still got my doubts about you."

"Just pull the damn lever."

Bishop fumbled for the release and a light lit up on the dash as the hatchback unlocked.

Ice crawled into the trunk with the two AKs. He positioned himself with his back wedged against the seat and his feet pressed into each corner. "Fuck, they're almost on us." He kicked the hatch up and unleashed with the assault rifle.

The rounds stitched the hood and windshield of the first Mercedes. It swerved violently but the driver managed to keep it on the road.

Ice gave it another burst as they rounded a bend but the bullets went wide.

A machine pistol appeared from the passenger window and Ice ducked as bullets thudded into the glass hatch, splintering shards over him.

"Shit, Ice, can't you do something about that?"

"How about you concentrate on going faster?" Ice yelled as he threw the empty AK at the Mercedes. It bounced off the hood and he picked up the second weapon hammering the windshield with a long burst.

The Mercedes jerked sideways, dove off the road, and flipped. It rolled over half a dozen times before coming to rest on its roof.

"Nice shooting tex!" yelled Bishop over the road noise and rushing wind.

"Don't get so excited, bro. There's another one and I'm down to my pistol." They overtook a car before rounding another bend, giving them precious seconds of respite.

The second sedan approached more cautiously than the first. Ice fired deliberate shots with his HK, trying to buy time. Men hung out of both of the rear windows with weapons. They fired long bursts of submachine gun fire at the little Toyota. Most of the bullets went wide, but a few thudded into the bodywork, narrowly missing Ice. He fired off the last of his rounds, crawled back to the cabin, and squeezed through to the passenger seat.

"Done, no more ammo."

"The radio, try the radio again," Bishop yelled over the gunfire and whine of the engine.

Ice could hear a faint voice and pulled out the radio, holding it to his ear.

"Beachcomber, this is Bella," the voice repeated, barely audible over the static.

"Bella, this is Comber, where the hell are you?" yelled Ice.

The voice became clearer; it was Vance. "Well, if that's you in a shitty toy car with the hatch sticking up being chased by the Mercs, we're about two miles in front of you."

Both men looked out to sea. Sure enough, in the distance they could make out a boat with a long wake trailing behind it.

Vance continued, "We're heading for a marina about four miles ahead of you, can you make it?"

More bullets hit the Prius. A round smashed the rearview mirror off the windshield.

"We'll be there," replied Ice.

Bishop jinked the little car from side to side as it sped down the highway, traffic becoming more frequent as they approached a township. They raced past a car coming the other way and danced in behind it, using it for cover.

The black Mercedes was relentless, weaving between the traffic to keep up, the gunmen looking for more opportunities to expend ammunition.

"I've got some bad news," said Bishop as he swerved around a bus. A truck filled the windshield. He swerved back into the other lane, narrowly missing the sixteen-wheeler.

"What?" Ice looked back through the open rear hatch. The Mercedes had misjudged the maneuver and had been forced off the highway onto the dirt median strip. It had bought them a few extra seconds.

"They've hit the tanks; we're running out of gas."

"How much battery power do we have?"

"Four bars. Do these things still run without fuel?" Bishop asked.

"Barely." Ice glanced back. "They're gaining on us again."

"We've got about a mile to go."

The Prius's engine blipped once and symbols lit up on the dashboard. "Oh, crap," said Bishop. "We're on electrics." He eased up on the pedal before stomping it to the floor. The little car lurched forward. "Come on, girl, bring it home."

The Mercedes was a hundred yards away when they

made the turn for the boating complex. The Prius's skinny tires skidded on the gravel, power faltering as Bishop tried to wring every last bit of energy from the batteries. They continued through the parking lot, narrowly missing a truck laden with Jet Skis.

They rolled onto the stone breakwater along the narrow gravel road that jutted into the sea. The Mercedes slowed now that its prey was trapped in the marina.

The end of the breakwater loomed. "Where the hell is the boat?" yelled Bishop.

"They'll be here."

Bishop jammed on the hand brake and slid the car to a halt across the track. Both PRIMAL operatives dove out of the car, hunkering behind it.

The Russians pulled up a short distance away, the doors flew open, and the gunmen opened fire with their pistols and submachine guns. Bullets hit the little Prius like a hailstorm and it shuddered under the fusillade of fire.

"We're fucked now." Bishop offered his hand to Ice. "Been a real pleasure."

Ice shook it. "It certainly has, bro."

The crack of high-velocity rounds interrupted the heartfelt moment. The gunfire hitting the Prius abruptly stopped and was replaced by the sound of eight hundred rounds a minute shredding the Mercedes sedan.

The *Princessa Bella* was still a couple of hundred yards away. Mitch's head and shoulders were poking out the front hatch at the bow where he was firing the MAG58 on a tripod. Tracer rounds streaked across the blue water of the Mediterranean and slammed into the Mercedes and the men around it. Full-metal-jacket rounds punched clean through the doors, tearing fist-sized holes as they exited. Flesh and metal were torn apart as the gun continued to hammer through a two-hundred-round belt. In less than a minute the car was a shredded wreck surrounded by the crumpled bodies of the Russian hit squad.

Vance brought the boat in fast, reversing the engines to kill off speed when he got within twenty feet of the break-water. In the bow Mitch kept the machine gun trained on the Russians.

"I'm afraid you're going to have to get a little wet," Vance yelled from the bridge of the vessel, the rocks of the breakwater preventing him from moving in closer.

"No problem." Ice pulled the remaining AK from the Prius and wiped it down with his T-shirt. He threw it into the water, dove in after it, and swam toward the boat.

Bishop wiped down the steering wheel and gear selector of the Prius, gave it a pat, and shrugged his jacket off as he walked down to the water's edge. He dove off a rock and swam after Ice toward the stern of the boat. As soon as they climbed aboard, Vance rammed the throttles forward and pointed the nose of the luxury cruiser toward Beirut.

KARELIN VILLA

"They're all dead, boss." The man Simeon had dispatched to check on the Spetsnaz team had returned. "One car was flipped over, no survivors. The other had been shot to pieces. Fucking disgusting."

Simeon was sitting at the table in the villa's dining room. There was no way he was going outside again, even after Aslan's bloated carcass was removed from the pool. He sat in silence contemplating his options.

"What do you want us to do?" the man asked.

"Get everyone packed," said Simeon. "We're going back to Russia. Tell the men in Dubai that we're pulling out."

"You sure, boss? I mean, that seems a little drastic."

"Are you a fucking moron? Did you see what those animals did to us? They came into our territory, infiltrated our base, and put a fucking bullet in Aslan. I'm now the head of this organization and I don't want to provoke people with that sort of capability! We go back to Russia, we lay low, and we find new territory to exploit, you hear me?"

"Yes, boss." The man scampered away.

Simeon poured himself a drink from one of the vodka bottles on the table. He wanted to get as far away as he could from Cyprus, from the UAE, and from the man whose voice would haunt his dreams for the rest of his life.

Chapter Twenty-One

PRIORITY MOVEMENTS AIRLIFT HANGAR

TARIQ WAS WAITING for them in the planning room. He had an icebox on the floor: Coronas, Bud Light, and Coopers Pale Ale were chilled and ready for consumption. There was a bottle of Mount Gay rum on the table and a glass.

"I thought you might enjoy a drink. You've certainly earned it," Tariq said as each of the team found a chair.

"I might pass," said Bishop. "I'm thinking I might lay off the booze for a little while. Those Russian alcoholics damn near killed me."

"You sure?" said Ice as he pulled out a Corona. "There seems to be some Aussie beer in here. Some cloudy crud called 'Coopers.'"

"Coopers! Here? You better not be messing with me."

Ice took one of the green-labeled beers and slid it across the table.

Bishop caught it. "Tariq, you've outdone yourself."

"You've earned it. The Karelin group closed up shop here this morning. All of them shipped out on a direct flight to Moscow. ADC has ceased all of their construction operations."

"So what happens to the guys in the camps?" Bishop asked as he downed a mouthful of beer.

"My people have taken over administration for the time being. All of them will be offered the opportunity for fair employment or a ticket home. One of my partner companies has placed a bid for all of ADC's construction projects."

"Better conditions, I hope."

"Of course. I have employees, Aden, not slaves."

"I don't doubt that at all; you've certainly looked after us so far. I'm just a bit disappointed we couldn't burn that entire organization to the ground."

"We need to pick our battles, Bish," said Vance. "Hit where we can have the biggest impact. We can't defeat every criminal and terrorist on the planet."

"We can have a damn good try," said Ice.

"You will need more people and better resources," said Tariq.

"Yeah, we need a permanent base of operations," added Vance. "Somewhere discreet. This hangar's a good staging area, but if we're going to get serious our people are going to need a place to train."

Tariq smiled. "I already have a location in mind. Some years ago Lascar Logistics purchased a small island in the South Pacific as a stopover and refueling facility. Since we switched to using longer-range aircraft the facility has been unused."

"If it's got an underground lair and a volcano, I'm in," Mitch joked.

"The Japanese used it as an airfield during World War Two. It has significant underground facilities."

"Wicked!" said the British technical guru. "Any chance you could fit an aircraft the size of an Ilyushin-76 in it?"

"What the hell are you planning?" asked Vance. "That's a goddamn strategic airlifter."

"Exactly. Imagine how many systems we could hide inside it. Boats are fun, old man, but an aircraft, well, there's nowhere they can't go. I've got this vision: a regular-looking cargo plane with the combined capabilities of a gunship, a surveillance platform, and a troop transporter."

"Sounds very expensive," said Vance.

The team all looked at Tariq, and he smiled. "No need to worry about that. My Lascar fleet has plenty of aircraft and our budget is extensive. There is adequate funding for additional equipment, personnel, and real estate." He got up from the table. "I'll leave you gentlemen to sort out the details of what you need."

The four PRIMAL operatives rose from the table and each shook hands with their benefactor. Once he was gone the room relaxed significantly.

"Top job, boys!" Vance raised his glass. "A few close calls, but all in all it went pretty much to plan."

Bishop grinned. "Speak for yourself. You didn't end up in a car chase and a gunfight all while nursing a ripper of a hangover."

"I also didn't lose a hundred K playing poker and tactically lodge myself under a two-grand-a-night hooker," shot back Vance.

"Good point; the job did come with certain perks."

They all laughed.

"OK, so what now?" asked Ice.

"Now we get real serious." Vance put his drink down.

"Chua gets in tomorrow; he's going to handle all intel, including the development of our HUMINT network. He's got contacts in the NSA, GCHQ, FAPSI... you name it. He'll be able to track down almost any target we want. Mitch, Ice, I want you two to follow up on the island that Tariq mentioned. Work out what we need to bring it up to a first-class training and operations facility. Bish, you and I are going on a recruiting drive."

"How long do you think it will take to get everything fully up and running?" Bishop asked.

"Could be six months, could be a year. Hard to say. Why? What's up? You got somewhere else to be?"

"Nope," said Bishop. "I'm just keen to start taking down bad guys."

Next in the PRIMAL Series

vinci-books.com/primal-unleashed

**A secret buried in the past. A mission to save the future.
A race against time. PRIMAL Unleashed.**

Turn the page for a free preview…

PRIMAL Unleashed: Prologue

Southern Afghanistan, 1989

The first mortar bombs dropped from the night sky directly inside the Russian platoon's defensive perimeter. The whistle of incoming projectiles sent men scurrying for cover, their survival instincts sharpened by three long years fighting the mujahideen. Captain Alexis Krijenko was sprinting for the nearest weapons pit when the barrage exploded, slamming him into the ground.

He shook his head to clear the shock. Strong hands grabbed his equipment harness, dragging him to the safety of a crudely constructed foxhole. A second barrage exploded, showering Krijenko with dirt as shrapnel sliced through the air inches above his skull. Crouching in the bottom of the pit, he faced Dostiger, the man who'd saved him. The Ukrainian laughed, his scarred and pitted face split into a psychotic grin.

"About time the Mooj found us, Captain!" Dostiger bellowed as more explosions filled the air with smoke and debris. "I thought they'd never come." The Spetsnaz platoon had waited all day but their adversaries were patient, holding off their attack until the sun had set behind the jagged mountaintops.

Krijenko's tired eyes met the manic stare of the Ukrainian. "They'll be on us within the hour, you crazy bastard."

"The Mooj want whatever's in that godforsaken hole, Captain," Dostiger yelled, gesturing toward the shaft carved into the heart of the mountain.

"No, comrade, they want our heads," he countered.

Dostiger's eyes grew even wider and his ugly grin more sadistic. "Fuck them! Let the filthy Muslims try. I'll send them to meet their prophet." He patted his Dragunov sniper rifle; the notches on its scarred wooden stock were too numerous to count and Krijenko knew that before long many more would join them.

———

Twelve hours earlier the Russian Spetsnaz platoon had been relocated from their usual hunting grounds in Helmand Province. They'd been driven east to Kandahar Airfield, a staging base for the withdrawal from Afghanistan. After ten years of brutal conflict, a ragtag army of mujahideen had defeated the mighty Russian war machine. Finally the men of the bloodied 40th Army could return home.

The sun sat low in the sky as Krijenko's men waited in the shell of a battle-scarred building, watching their comrades depart in a continuous stream of massive Antonov transport aircraft. They looked on blankly as the long lines of soldiers edged toward the departure point. Meanwhile Dostiger dozed, slumped against his equipment.

Eyes bloodshot and skin gray from exhaustion, Krijenko

managed a haggard smile as a line of regular troops ran forward eagerly, waved on board by a young, fresh-faced officer armed with a clipboard.

Finally it was their turn. Krijenko surged forward with his men. They almost reached the line when the clipboard-wielding officer stopped them.

He couldn't believe it. It was their turn to depart, but his war-weary Spetsnaz platoon was being waved to another holding area. His soldiers stared angrily as another group took their place. No warning, no explanation; the young officer simply handed him a set of orders and waved his clipboard toward a pair of waiting Mi-17 transport helicopters. They wouldn't be going home.

Demoralized they hauled their equipment across to the helicopters and began stowing their heavy-weapons and boxes of ammunition. They were interrupted by a helmet-clad loadmaster.

"Personal weapons only," he yelled into Krijenko's ear over the increasing scream of the helicopter's twin turbines. "High-altitude flight, comrade. Leave anything you can. If we're too heavy, then…" He gestured with his gloved hand, chopping at his neck.

Krijenko scowled as his men discarded their heavy weapons, piling the grenade launchers, machine guns, and mortars on the tarmac. These weapons had given the Spetsnaz a distinct advantage over the mujahideen.

Once the platoon was on board, the two helicopters took off, circling Kandahar before heading north. Krijenko noted the absence of the attack helicopter escort that usually accompanied all air movement in Afghanistan. An ominous sign that this was no regular mission. Krijenko kept his concerns to himself as they gained altitude. His men were veterans and he had earned their trust. They would follow him on any mission, no matter how bone-tired and no matter what the odds. He watched them, one by one, dip their heads as the thud of the rotors and vibration of the aircraft lulled them to sleep. Battle-hardened, they had long ago learned to rest whenever the opportunity arose.

Dostiger peered with anticipation through the plastic bubble window, the sun-faded dome morphing the barren rocky ridges and green valleys below into an alien environment. For three years this mountainous terrain had been his home; a harsh and unforgiving place that had claimed the lives of thousands of invaders. It was a land of warriors: Mongol, Persian, British, and now Russian blood had soaked this soil. For the Ukrainian it had become a hunting ground. At last count he had sent one hundred and seventy mujahideen to meet their maker, and now whatever god was watching over him had given him the opportunity to make it an even two hundred.

Dostiger smiled sadistically as he looked back at the platoon dozing in the belly of the helicopter. They wanted to go home, but not him. Something in the depths of his soul told him that this was where he was supposed to be. In these rugged mountains he would find his destiny.

A change in the pitch of the rotors woke the rest of the platoon. The scream of the turbines rose, the helicopter approaching ceiling height.

The loadmaster held up two fingers to indicate two minutes out. All signs of sleep gone, the men checked weapons, tightened equipment, and prepared for potential combat. Their eyes were alert, bodies tensed and ready.

Krijenko's steely gaze locked onto the window. The rocky crags looked close enough to touch but nothing seemed familiar about this area. His men would not have the advantage of knowing the ground. Nor would they have the reassurance of heavy weapons and air support. He looked back and met Dostiger's stare. The mad Ukrainian smiled.

The helicopter shuddered as it clawed its way upward to a flat clearing on the side of a barren mountain. With a final lurch it cleared the razor edge and descended onto a roughly constructed landing zone. The clamshell rear doors swung open as it hit the ground and the loadmaster frantically waved them clear. The men fanned out, weapons ready, eyes scanning for any possible threat. They found cover behind boulders and in folds of the earth, encircling the aircraft as its rotors idled.

Krijenko stepped off onto the windswept mountain, crouched, and rapidly assessed the terrain. The landing zone was large, easily accommodating the two helicopters. It was dominated on three sides by jagged ridgelines and rocky outcrops, while at the lower end a rudimentary road snaked away to the south. Parallel to the road, large boulders and deep gullies would allow any enemy a protected approach. Krijenko spat into the dust as he stared at the terrain; experience told him he lacked the manpower to defend this ground.

He gave a nod to let his team leaders know they had positioned their men well, before his eyes were drawn to an open pair of giant blast doors set into the mountainside. The entrance leered at him like a gaping mouth. Around the doors a small team of army engineers was rigging explosive charges. They were preparing to seal the tunnel.

An officer walked around the idling aircraft to Krijenko. Everything about the man screamed military intelligence, from his swagger to the long leather jacket that flapped in the wind, snapping against his black boots. Krijenko rose and stood to meet him face-to-face.

"Captain," the intelligence major said curtly. "Captain, you will hold this position until the engineers are ready to seal the shaft."

A question formed on Krijenko's lips, but the superior officer cut him short.

"No questions. The mission is simple. Keep the Muslim rabble away until our men seal the shaft." He gestured to the engineers, still busy at work. "This facility must not fall into the hands of the mujahideen. God help you if you fail."

Without waiting for a reply the man turned on his heel and joined a line of civilians as they scurried out the tunnel into the waiting helicopters. Krijenko noted the fear etched on their pasty white faces. These were noncombatants, men who were supposed to be kept far from the reaches of the enemy.

As the scientists hurried into the rear of the helicopters, the intelligence officer paused in a side door and looked back over his shoulder at the Spetsnaz platoon. Krijenko thought he saw the slightest trace of pity, then the hatch slammed shut and he was gone.

The doors on both helicopters closed and Krijenko turned back to where the engineers were busy moving explosives into the shaft. Brown wooden boxes were stacked ten high. Enough explosives to bring down a mountain.

The scream of turbines snapped his attention back to the helicopters beating their blades as they lifted off. Stones, flung like shrapnel, pelted the soldiers as the rotor wash tore across the landing zone. The thumping cadence of the choppers faded into the wide expanse of the Afghan sky.

The mountain fell silent. Krijenko, his platoon, and a team of army engineers were alone.

———

The Soviet High Command had not expected the mujahideen to advance so quickly. Driven by a ruthless commander, they had surged south with a determined focus, moving heavy weapons on the backs of mules and horses. Familiar with the terrain, their scouts located Krijenko's platoon without being spotted. Mortars and heavy machine guns had been carried up the steep ridge-lines in silence, crews sighting the weapons with deadly efficiency. As the sun fell below the horizon and darkness set in, they attacked.

The Spetsnaz soldiers defended their positions desperately throughout the night. Mortar and rocket fire was unrelenting, the flashing explosions cutting down five of Krijenko's best men. Stripped of weapons and ammunition, their bodies lay face down to the rear of the fighting positions, blood soaking into the hard earth. Three furious assaults from separate sides had been repulsed and as dawn approached, the platoon was exhausted and low on ammunition.

Krijenko shrugged off the sense of futility as he crouched in a hastily dug weapons pit scraped from the rocky ground by bare hands and bayonets. His two remaining team leaders and the commander of the engineer detachment were huddled next to him. Their tired eyes nervously scanned the perimeter, vigilant for the next enemy attack.

The young engineer faced Krijenko and spoke rapidly.

"Comrade, my men have prepared all the explosives and we're ready to seal the shaft."

Dostiger, the Ukrainian team leader, leaned in toward him, his rank breath revolting the engineer. "What the hell is in there?" He gestured toward the shaft, barely visible in the early-morning twilight.

"I don't know. They didn't tell us," the engineer stammered. "My, my orders were simple; bury it so it can't be found." The young man refused to look at Dostiger's pockmarked face; the ugly Ukrainian terrified him. "It's something they don't want the Mooj to have. I don't know."

Dostiger stared at the open shaft and his brow furrowed. "We should check it out, Captain. It could be worth something."

Krijenko shook his head. "My orders are to seal it, Dostiger, and seal it I will." He looked back at the engineer. "Go. Do it!"

The young man hurried back to the opening where his two remaining sappers were laying the final lengths of slow-burn fuse. He was eager to finish the job before the sun rose over the horizon and exposed his men to the mujahideen positioned along the dominant ridgelines. Already the sky was glowing with the approaching dawn.

As the engineers lit the fuse, mortar rounds pounded the landing zone in a fearsome barrage. The lethal bombs slayed another four Spetsnaz soldiers, their bodies shredded by the shrapnel that lashed their fighting positions.

As the engineers sprinted from the shaft across the open ground of the landing zone, a DSHK heavy machine gun opened up from one of the surrounding ridgelines. 12.7mm high-velocity rounds riddled their bodies, hydrostatic shock destroying flesh and shattering bones, ripping the men to pieces. They were dead before they hit the ground.

The Afghan skirmishers advanced, flitting from cover to cover as their fire-support positions suppressed the Spetsnaz platoon. Krijenko, manning a dead soldier's machine gun, worked feverishly to hold off the mujahideen, but one by one his men fell silent as they succumbed to the relentless onslaught. He watched a grenade detonate in Dostiger's position. The mad Ukrainian was thrown clear, one leg torn and bloodied.

The barrel of the machine gun glowed red as Krijenko pumped the trigger, sending short bursts lancing into the advancing fighters. The last belt of ammunition disappeared in a final burst and the gun fell silent, the bolt slamming forward on an empty chamber. Krijenko reached into his chest harness and drew a pistol, leveling it at the Afghan warrior running at him. His first round entered the man's head below the cheek and blew out the back of his skull. There was no second bullet.

Krijenko never saw the fighter who shot him in the neck. The projectile ripped through the spine, killing him instantly. The pistol fell from his hand and he collapsed. As the first drops of the Russian officer's blood soaked into the ground, the earth erupted, throwing his body into the air. The explosives detonated along fault lines, causing thousands of tons of rock to collapse into the shaft. A blast wave of dust and rubble blew out from the mountainside, sweeping the forward line of mujahideen fighters from their feet. The engineers had done their job well.

As the dust settled on the bloodied bodies of the slain Spetsnaz, the Afghan warriors regrouped; their heavy-weapons teams filtering down from the high ground to join the assaulting force. They moved out of the shadows and began searching the Russian defensive positions, stripping the corpses of valuables. A tall figure strode through the scavengers, his white robes unmarked by the dust and smoke of the battlefield.

The man's dark eyes stared intently at the wall of rock that denied him his goal. Frustration momentarily passed over his hard features and he turned away, distracted by the moans of a bloodied and broken body that lay at his feet. One of the Afghan fighters drew a wicked-looking blade and raised it back in a sweeping arc, ready to dispatch the casualty.

"Wait," the white-robed leader demanded. He knelt down next to the wounded man, his Russian halting but clear. "What was hidden here?"

Dostiger smiled and chuckled. "You and I, we will never know." The Ukrainian was delirious from loss of blood and the morphine injection he'd stabbed into his thigh.

The Afghan grunted stiffly and leaned closer. "You will die here, Russian."

Dostiger's grin widened and blood dribbled from his lips, staining his fatigues. He laughed manically. "We all die, comrade. How many of your fighters will I join in hell?"

The mujahideen commander stared at Dostiger's face before he rose and turned to the fighter next to him. "Find a stretcher. The fearless one comes with us."

PRIMAL Unleashed: Chapter One

WESTERN HIGHLANDS, SIERRA LEONE, 2000

A white UN Land Rover and a battered Bedford truck slowly wound their way along a narrow dirt road in the western highlands of Sierra Leone. The vehicles pushed on through the overgrown vines and saplings, the African jungle's attempts to reclaim the track. The earthy smell of rotting leaves filled the air and sprawling trees blocked the sunlight, spawning growths of moss and fungi.

An Australian officer, Lieutenant Aden Bishop, rode in the front of the Land Rover next to the driver, a young Sierra Leone soldier. Behind him, Colonel Kapur reclined in the backseat. Although the Indian UN officer was technically in command, he was content to let Bishop take charge. Their mission was to inspect the Kilimi refugee camp, a routine undertaking that the colonel would not normally participate in. He had only volunteered for the short-notice tasking to impress the UN military commander. Usually he preferred to remain in Sierra Leone's capital, Freetown, relaxing in the air-conditioning of the UN headquarters.

Trailing the four-wheel drive, the Bedford truck transported ten Indian UN soldiers perched on its hard wooden benches. Well-armed and enthusiastic, the peacekeepers had excellent discipline, which made up for their limited training. Clad in their heavy khaki uniforms and light-blue berets, they silently endured the stifling heat of the canvas-topped truck, the ancient suspension amplifying every bump.

The diesel engines of the convoy bellowed as the drivers pushed them hard, climbing the slippery track toward Kilimi. Native birds were startled from the trees and larger animals crashed through the heavy undergrowth to escape the noisy intruders. Every few miles the two vehicles passed small villages unmarked on the map.

Bishop squinted as the morning sun streamed through gaps in the thick jungle canopy, raising the humidity to oppressive levels. He removed his UN beret to wipe his brow, and checked the map. The young Australian officer struggled to navigate in the dense jungle; the huge trees that punched up through the shadowy undergrowth filled the sky with a wall of greenery, blocking out the view and making it impossible to identify any useful landmarks.

As they drove past yet another isolated village, Bishop's driver pointed out a cluster of ramshackle huts. "Sir, my grandfather was born there." Chickens scratched in the mud around one of the rusted corrugated-iron walls. Looking across at the lieutenant the driver smiled. "I know this area well, sir. I won't get you lost."

"I'm not worried about that, Erasto," Bishop said as he looked up from the map. "I'm more worried about how far the militias are from the camp." His brow furrowed as his thoughts turned to another refugee camp at Songo. A rogue RUF militia had attacked it only two weeks earlier and a UN patrol had watched helplessly as the refugees were hacked to pieces. The peacekeepers' orders forbade them to fire except in self-defence.

After the incident Bishop had been sent to Songo to provide a detailed report. Over a hundred refugees had been maimed or slaughtered; the smell of the rotting corpses was still fresh in his mind.

The young driver continued, "Well, usually many RUF in this area but now most have gone."

"Most?"

"Yes, sir. Some are still here but not many. Most have gone back to their villages. Only some criminals remain, but they will be afraid of us."

Bishop was skeptical. He knew the drug-fueled militias were not easily deterred. To make matters worse the team was babysitting a ranking UN officer, a tempting target for kidnapping.

Colonel Kapur leaned forward to tap Bishop on the shoulder. "You can tell the young private not to worry; a section of Indian infantry is more than enough to deal with a handful of criminals."

Bishop clenched his jaw and kept his eyes fixed on the road ahead. The sheer arrogance of the colonel disgusted him; the man wouldn't directly address the private who was their full-time driver. It was below his status to talk to an enlisted soldier, and a native one at that.

Kapur continued, "This is your first real mission, is it not, Lieutenant?"

"Yes, sir, that's correct," Bishop responded curtly.

"Well, I've served with the UN a number of times. I have also led missions against the rebels in Kashmir.

Considering your inexperience you are lucky that I chose to accompany this mission."

"Very lucky, sir."

The colonel took it as a compliment, sat back, and began studying his own map.

What a cock, thought Bishop. This man clearly has more experience drinking coffee than commanding soldiers. The overweight colonel even had the audacity to wear his dress uniform in the field. The buttons on the sweat-stained shirt strained against his protruding belly. With all his ribbons and braid he looked more like a bandmaster than a soldier.

Despite the presence of the pompous colonel, Bishop was enjoying his first deployment. He appreciated the multi-national aspects of working with the UN, and as a junior officer he was gaining valuable experience operating in a high-threat environment.

The dangers that lurked in the surrounding terrain weren't obvious as the convoy made their way through the thick green vegetation of Kilimi National Park. As they passed through villages, young men and women spilled out of their huts, happily waving at the passing soldiers. It was only their handless limbs and scarred bodies that hinted at the inhumane crimes that had occurred here and the threat still posed by the roaming militias.

The UN has failed these people, reflected Bishop.

A young boy grinned at him, waving vigorously as the Land Rover crawled past. Leaning against a crude crutch, the boy's right leg was missing from the knee down. The soldier in Bishop wanted to hunt down and tear out the throats of the animals who had perpetrated the act, but the UN rules of engagement forbade him. In the back of his mind he doubted his ability to follow this directive. What kind of man could stand by and watch these RUF bastards hack the limbs from children, he rationalized.

Bishop checked his map again. They had almost reached the refugee camp and had encountered no sign of recent militia activity. Was it possible the RUF fighters were actually abiding by the guidelines laid down in the cease-fire? Bishop remained wary. Many of the RUF were no more than criminals and a refugee camp was easy pickings for heavily armed thugs.

The road narrowed even further. They inched forward over a simple log bridge and continued up into the high-lands. Thick red clay caked the tires, and the drivers strug-gled to keep from sliding off the crude path and down the steep embankment into the green abyss below.

Bishop looked up as the Land Rover slowed. Spotting something ahead, the driver dropped down a gear. In the distance two armed men were standing in front of a battered white pickup parked across the track. A third was manning a heavy machine gun mounted on the truck.

"Looks like trouble, sir." The young driver sounded worried.

"It's OK, Erasto. It's probably just some of the local militia," Bishop reassured the nervous youth. "Pull over and we'll sort this out." The UN officer was only a few years older than his driver, but his confidence and training gave him a leadership presence that belied his age.

They slowed to a halt. Bishop opened the Land Rover's battered door and stepped down. His boots sank into the mud. A cloud of mosquitoes swarmed up from septic puddles of water. He swatted them casually, the mud and insects barely registering. His mind focused on the potential threat posed by the armed men.

The sound of squelching boots behind him drew his

attention and he turned to face the Indian section commander.

"Doesn't look good, sir," said Corporal Mirza Mansoor.

"I hear you, Mirza," Bishop replied quietly, his hand instinctively moving to the holster on his hip.

"A very dangerous position, sir," Mirza said, matter-of-factly. The Indian's hard Asiatic features displayed no emotion.

"Yeah, we're wedged in pretty tight. If they arc up with that machine gun, we're cactus," Bishop muttered. Beads of perspiration ran down his face.

"Do you think they are RUF?"

"Maybe, maybe not. Could be locals."

"Well, sir, whoever they are, they don't look friendly."

"They're certainly not a reception party, that's for sure," Bishop agreed.

"What do you want us to do?"

From the backseat of the Land Rover, Colonel Kapur interrupted, speaking through the open window. "Corporal, the RUF wouldn't dare come into the exclusion zone during the cease-fire. These men here must be locals and there are only three of them. We will simply approach and discuss our access to the Kilimi camp."

Bishop glanced down at the senior officer and nodded. "The colonel is probably right."

Mirza raised an eyebrow.

Bishop continued. "Odds are they're just trying to make a few dollars by charging the refugees passage. We should be able to bribe our way through the checkpoint."

Mirza pointed up the road at the vehicle. "Do you want me to take some of the men up there and find out what they want?"

Kapur made to speak but Bishop interrupted him. "No, the colonel and I will go talk to them."

"OK, sir, we will be ready."

"Good. Tell your men to stay with the vehicles but be prepared to follow us up. The last thing we want to do is provoke a bunch of trigger-happy militia." He pointed out their current location on the map. "If they won't let us through, the camp is only on the other side of this crest. We can always double back and approach along one of these tracks with a recon party." Bishop had worked with Mirza for barely a month but already he trusted the Indian corporal. Everything about the smaller man inspired confidence, from his well-pressed uniform and immaculately cleaned rifle to his steady, almost icy demeanor. Even the thin mustache was fitting in an old-school way; he was a born soldier and Bishop had no doubt the blood of India's fiercest warriors ran strong in his veins.

"Understood, sir." Mirza gave a nod and headed back to his men. The other nine soldiers had already dismounted and were dispersed in the dense foliage either side of the track.

Bishop opened the rear door of the Land Rover and Kapur reluctantly pried his rotund body from the seat. A twitch appeared at the corner of the senior officer's eye as he stepped into the mud. "It might be better for me to stay with the vehicle," he said. "We don't want to appear overly intimidating to these men."

No chance of that, thought Bishop, you look like the Indian version of Elton John. "Should be OK, sir. They'll probably respect an officer of your rank."

"Yes, good point, lieutenant," Kapur replied unconvincingly, adjusting the beret perched on his bald, perspiring head.

They walked steadily uphill toward the checkpoint, two figures in stark contrast. The corpulent colonel in dress uniform waddled behind Bishop's athletic frame clad in distinctive Australian combat fatigues.

As they drew closer, Bishop saw the gunmen were only teenagers. They all wore grubby, torn jeans, and sported the usual talismans and charms to ward off bullets. He smiled grimly as he noticed one of them wearing a bright-red life jacket over his bare torso; some of the Africans had strange ideas regarding protective equipment.

The tallest of the boys was leaning against the hood of the vehicle, a cigarette hanging limply from his mouth. He waited until the approaching UN officers were only a few steps away, then jerked upright, hefted a G3 assault rifle, and gestured to his comrades. The shorter boy, who was casually cradling an AK-47, stepped forward and slowly raised his hand. The third swiveled the heavy machine gun toward them from the back of the rusted pickup.

Bishop stopped only a few paces away. He was close enough to notice their eyes were glazed, and slid his hand to the grip of the Browning 9mm nestled against his hip. It was the norm for UN officers to carry only handguns, but faced with three heavily armed gunmen, Bishop wished he'd insisted on being issued a rifle. He carefully positioned himself a few paces back from the Colonel, slightly out of the immediate firing line, aware that drugs and alcohol could result in unpredictable behavior.

A sideways glance at the battered Toyota pickup caused Bishop's stomach to lurch. Jammed onto the spike of a snapped side mirror was a severed human head. Flies crawled into the open eyes and a black bloated tongue protruded between decaying lips. The putrid smell assaulted the young lieutenant's senses and he struggled to keep his composure, the taste of bile filling his mouth.

All three gunmen stared intently at the gold braid decorating Colonel Kapur's uniform, like children intrigued by the costume of a clown. The tall youth with the cigarette stepped forward confidently, pointing at Kapur.

"You some kinda big boss man?" He reeked of alcohol and unwashed sweat. "My name is General Terminator!" The young African stabbed a thumb into his bare chest, then swept his arms wide. "An dis here area is under control of dah West Side Boys!"

The hairs on Bishop's neck rose. He realized the checkpoint could only mean one thing; the rest of the gang was already in the refugee camp. It was going to be the Songo massacre all over again.

The youths were members of one of the most feared RUF groups in Sierra Leone, a gang that raped pregnant women and sliced open their bellies to gamble on the sex of the unborn child.

Kapur froze, unable to respond, much to the amusement of the West Side Boys. "Who is da big boss now, man? Run back to your mama before the Terminator kill you all!" the gunman screamed. He was completely unintimidated, his ego fueled by the UN officer's fear and a cocktail of alcohol and drugs.

Bishop stepped closer to the colonel. "We just need to get to the camp," he stated, keeping his fists clenched to stop his hands from shaking.

The leader of the trio spat at him. "Fuck off, you white Yankee fuck. You not going anywhere."

Before Bishop could respond, Kapur grasped his arm, pulling him away. "We need to go now, lieutenant."

Bishop lowered his voice, "Sir, I am going to offer them a bribe. It might change their minds."

"No, Lieutenant Bishop. You will—"

Sharp, rapid cracks of gunfire in the distance cut him off and his eyes grew wide. More bursts of automatic fire were accompanied by screams and shouts.

The West Side Boys started whooping, jumping up and down, and punching their weapons in the direction of the refugee camp. They laughed, making crude gestures at the colonel. "Don't be afraid, big boss. We will save some of da young girls for you."

Rage and shame boiled up in Bishop as he imagined the RUF gang storming through the camp, raping women and mutilating men. Images of the aftermath of the Songo massacre flashed through his mind.

Stepping behind the petrified colonel to block the boys' view, he disengaged his pistol holster's thumb-brake. Grabbing Kapur roughly by the front of his shirt, he pulled him close enough to smell the rancid stench of the man's sweat.

"I'll shoot you myself if you try to stop me. Now give me the cash," Bishop snarled. The colonel looked stunned. Hand shaking, he pulled a thick yellow envelope from his pocket and passed it to the Australian.

Bishop caught the eye of Mirza, who was cautiously walking up the muddy track. He gave the Indian a sly hand signal and turned to face the crazed gunmen. They were laughing with each other, excited at the prospect of joining the action.

Bishop's confidence drained away as he assessed the situation. Deep in his gut he knew it was too risky to try to negotiate with 'General Terminator'; the mix of drugs and alcohol in the youth's bloodstream would make him irrational and impulsive. Clammy with sweat, he wiped his right hand on his pants. His chest tightened, constricting his breathing.

Swallowing nervously, he forced himself to address the young gunman. "Please, General Terminator, what is happening? Who is firing?" Bishop meekly moved closer, his left hand waving the wad of US currency to draw his attention. "Can we pay you to get through to the camp?"

"I told you to fuck off, Yankee. Take your fucking money and go home before I cut off your hands as well!" Terminator cackled like a jackal, turning back to grin at his two comrades. "Short sleeves or long sleeves?" He laughed at the joke, enjoying the attention of being the big man.

Bishop realized in a panic that he'd misjudged the situation. Armed with only a pistol he was faced off against three RUF fighters with automatic weapons.

Terminator's expression abruptly became serious and he swung his rifle toward Bishop. Cocking it, his voice took on a savage tone. "Go home, Yankee pig, or General Terminator will blow your head off and fuck you right up!"

Bishop tensed as the G3 pointed directly at him. In his mind he could see the bullet leaving the barrel and burying itself in his stomach. The youth looked back toward his companions, and Bishop snapped. He leaped forward, pushing the barrel of the rifle away from his body, and in one smooth action drew his pistol from its holster. The Browning barked twice in quick succession, the 9mm rounds smashing into Terminator's sternum, ripping through his heart, blowing its remains out through the back of his rib cage. The teenager toppled back into the mud, a look of shock on his face. A choking sound came from his throat as his shattered lungs filled with blood.

Bishop had never shot anyone before, but the severity of the act didn't have time to register. Without thinking he adopted a two-handed grip and adjusted his aim to target the second youth who was bringing his rifle up. The fore sight and rear sight aligned on the gunman's head. Bishop fired rapidly. Two rounds went wide but the third penetrated the teen's skull, spraying his brain across the side of the battered Toyota pickup, streaks of blood and gray matter blending with the rust.

The blast of Mirza's AK-47 snapped Bishop out of his instinctive shooting as the third gunman was blown over the tailgate of the Toyota, his red life jacket shredded by the bullets. The Indian moved forward deliberately, his AK-47 tight against his shoulder, alert to the possibility of additional fighters.

"Are they all dead, sir?" Mirza asked as he pushed past the pickup to scan the jungle ahead.

"Yeah, you did well, corporal," Bishop replied, trying to sound confident. "There were only three of them."

He holstered his pistol and knelt next to the corpse of Terminator, hands shaking as he checked the G3 rifle and stripped ammunition from the body. Bishop avoided looking at the lifeless face. This kid should be in school, he thought. What the fuck was he doing out here? What was he doing with a gang of animals like the West Side Boys? Did I have to shoot him? He shook his head and buried the thoughts; now was not the time for questions. He was now committed to saving the refugees even if it meant more killing.

Bishop was aware he was blatantly breaching his rules of engagement. The UN mandate hammered through this brain, again and again, the inhumane futility of it. In the distance a woman screamed. A long, shrill scream. Fuck this! he thought and hurried back to the UN vehicles with Terminator's rifle and ammunition.

PRIMAL Unleashed: Chapter Two

KILIMI REFUGEE CAMP

Colonel Kapur stood in shock as Bishop sorted his equipment on the hood of the Land Rover. Checking his map, he identified a concealed route into the refugee camp and stuffed the document into his thigh pocket. He swiftly stripped the battered G3 assault rifle he'd taken from Terminator's corpse, checking its serviceability. As he methodically inspected the components, Mirza and two of the other soldiers approached.

Bishop scrutinized the rifle as he spoke, "You know what I have to do."

"Yes, sir," Mirza murmured, glancing over at the colonel, then back to Bishop.

"I can't ask you to come."

"Three of us will go with you. The others will stay here and look after the colonel and the driver."

"Be ready to move in two minutes."

Bishop reassembled the rifle, satisfied that it would work

reliably. He slammed home a magazine and cocked it, placing the other four magazines into the pockets of his shirt and pants. This is the first and last time I go outside the wire without body armor and a rifle, he told himself. Hastily, he tied a short length of cord around the stock of the weapon, allowing it to hang from his shoulder. Finally, he changed the magazine in his pistol and reholstered it. Ready for action, he glanced at the colonel and tossed the thick wad of bribe money to him.

"Stay here, sir. If we don't come back within the hour, leave for Freetown."

Kapur nodded, horrified at the calm demeanor of the young man who had just slain two teenage gunmen. It was clear what Aden was going to do next.

Bishop gathered Mirza and the two other soldiers in front of the Bedford truck. "OK, men, we don't have much time." Gunshots still echoed intermittently from the direction of the camp, and ominously, the screaming had stopped. "We're going to the camp and we'll do whatever we must to protect the refugees. Do you understand?"

"Yes, sir," they replied in unison.

Bishop looked the group over and continued. "I appreciate you all backing me up." When this was over, Bishop knew that Colonel Kapur would most likely punish them.

"Sir, we wouldn't let you go on your own."

Bishop gave Mirza a nod, then pulled out his map. "Alright, we're going to move down this track through the jungle, avoiding the main road. Stay with me, I'll lead. Understood?"

"Yes, sir."

"Alright, job's on, let's roll."

Bishop, weapon held ready, moved swiftly along the steep track, sliding through the dark soil and rotting leaf litter. The three other men kept pace, patrolling silently behind him.

At the bottom of the slope they splashed through a shallow creek before coming to the edge of the jungle. As they reached the thick bushes bordering the camp, they crouched, watching for movement. The first ramshackle wooden huts and white triangular UNHCR tents looked deserted. Behind them, row after row of similar dilapidated shelters stretched for over five hundred yards, bounded on one side by the jungle and on the other by a dirty brown waterway littered with rubbish and plastic containers. In the distance Bishop could make out the hazy green mountains of Guinea, a safe haven for the antigovernment militias.

More screaming echoed through the empty camp. He signaled the men to move in. "Listen up. I'm on point; you cover the flanks and the rear." He used his finger to draw their positions in the dirt. In diamond formation they could deal with a threat from any direction.

"I want the bastards dead: no prisoners, no wounded—dead!" Bishop's hushed voice was sharp with anger and the Indian soldiers all nodded nervously. "Alright, men, let's do this."

The small team pushed out from the foliage, cautiously moving across the bare ground to the camp. The fetid stench of human refuse and rotting garbage hit them as they reached the first line of patchwork tents. Carefully stepping over piles of rubbish, they kept their rifles ready, eyes continually scanning.

As they penetrated deeper into the camp, the conditions worsened. Bishop noticed bullet holes in a sheet of corrugated iron used to patch a hut; the blood splattered across it looked fresh. The distant screams and yelling grew louder as they advanced. A women's terrified shrieks were punctuated by gunshots.

Bishop signaled a halt. He crept forward, looking for a vantage point to observe the center of the camp. As he stepped across a narrow drainage ditch, the soft dirt gave way, dumping his boot in raw sewage splashing it up his leg. He swore as he clambered out of the mess and into an abandoned hut. Crouching, he peered between two sheets of rusted iron.

Not more than thirty yards from him, ten RUF fighters had herded a nearly a hundred refugees into the clearing. Huddled on their knees in the mud, the men, women, and children looked like terrified animals waiting to be slaughtered. Some wept silently. Others clutched each other with skinny arms, eyes wide with fear.

Scattered about the group were mutilated bodies. Drenched with blood and missing limbs, the corpses were a savage warning against resistance. To the side was a bloodied pile of amputated arms and legs.

Unaware of the demise of their sentries, the gunmen screamed with lung-bursting ferocity, fired their weapons into the air, and lashed out at the prisoners. Bishop watched as two young gang members dragged a screaming woman into a blue UN medical aid tent. "Bastards," he muttered through gritted teeth.

Two more RUF trained their weapons on the wide-eyed refugees while the others gathered around a huge man wielding a machete. My god, Bishop thought. He's a bloody giant. The RUF commander moved like a predator. His scars marked him as a veteran killer; old gunshot wounds disfigured his bare muscled torso and a vicious scar twisted around his throat. His clothes reflected his status, the closest to any form of military uniform worn by the gang. Camouflage pants were tucked into a shiny pair of black jungle boots and a tangle of talismans dangled from his neck. The ensemble was topped by a dirty blue UN beret.

The RUF fighters gathered around their leader, cheering as he waved the bloodstained machete above his head. He grabbed a young boy and pinned him face down in the mud. He rammed his boot into the child's back so his arms splayed out on either side.

Bishop was transfixed on the grisly scene. He knew exactly what was about to happen but couldn't move. Fear paralyzed him.

The commander's biceps bulged and he swung the blade like a broadsword. The machete sliced through the skinny arm with a sickening crunch of bone, burying itself in the thick red mud. The boy's blood-curdling scream came to an abrupt halt as he fainted.

Retrieving the severed arm, the big man held it high for the terrified refugees to see. Spittle sprayed from his mouth as he raged, "You spineless bastards, we fight for your freedom and you force us to do this!" He flung the arm into the growing pile of limbs, a thick cloud of flies lifting from the congealed, bloodied flesh as it landed with a wet thud.

Bishop collapsed to his knees. Vomit sprayed from his mouth, his body wracked with dry heaves and eyes filled with tears. He didn't notice Mirza enter the hut; it took a firm grip on his arm to snap him out of shock.

"Sir, sir, are you OK?" Mirza whispered.

Shame gave way to fury as he wiped his mouth.

"I'm fine." Bishop wiped the tears from his eyes and looked up. His teeth clenched. "Are the men ready?"

Mirza nodded confidently and led him out of the derelict hut where his men waited.

Bishop exhaled. "Let's do this."

They advanced into the clearing with Bishop in the lead. His rifle barked savagely as he concentrated fire on the startled group of RUF. High-velocity bullets tore into the bodies of the gunmen, rending flesh and shattering bone. The three Indian AK-47s roared, laying down automatic fire in support of Bishop's single shots.

The leader dove to the ground at the first sign of the troops, evading the deadly hail of bullets that ripped through his followers. Frantically he crawled behind the closest line of shelters.

Catching a glimpse of the fleeing boss, Bishop charged forward, his weapon blazing until the breech locked open on an empty magazine. He dropped the smoking rifle, the sling around his shoulder caught it as he drew his pistol, cutting down another gunman in a volley of bullets. The RUF fighter collapsed backward as Bishop emptied the entire magazine into his chest.

The dying man's ugly features contorted in pain. A frothy mixture of blood and mucus dribbled from his lips.

Bishop slammed a fresh magazine into his Browning, and with a loud slap, released the slide, chambering a round. He casually raised the pistol and shot the man cleanly through the forehead.

Eight of the gang members lay mortally wounded or dead as a result of the fusillade of fire laid down by the UN peacekeepers. Two of them were riddled with bullets, their pants around their ankles. They would never rape another woman.

The RUF commander had fled with one of his men into the depths of the camp. Bishop gave chase, striding away from the twitching corpse. As he picked up the pace he holstered his pistol and changed the magazine on his rifle.

"Wait for us!" Mirza yelled.

Bishop sprinted through the empty camp, ears ringing from the gunfight. "Where is that son of a bitch?" he muttered. Running between the threadbare tents, he caught a glimpse of movement ahead. Instinctively he dropped, skidding through a pile of trash. A volley of bullets cracked through the air above him. Rolling sideways, he pumped the trigger of his rifle, the rounds smashing into the firer's position, spraying it with splinters of wood.

The shooter exposed his body for a split second as he sought cover. It was enough time for Bishop to snap off a single aimed shot instantly dropping the gunman. The corpse continued forward under its own momentum, slamming through the flimsy wall of a hut.

Bishop edged forward, his sights focused on the crumpled wall. Movement flashed to the left. He whipped round.

The massive RUF commander bore down on him screaming and swinging a machete. Bishop blocked the blade with his rifle. The force jarred the weapon from his hands and snapped the improvised sling. He lashed out with a fist but the blow bounced off the man's face, the impact jarring his wrist.

In one smooth motion the African reversed his strike, punching the handle of the machete into Bishop's gut, driving the air from his lungs and catapulting him onto his back.

The machete flashed down again and buried itself into the thick red clay. Bishop rolled and snatched the Browning from its holster. The muscular African moved faster. He kicked the pistol away and pounced, swinging the machete down. Bishop caught a wrist with both hands. The veins in the commander's forearm bulged as his brute force and weight pushed the blade down.

Bishop felt a strong hand grasp his throat, closing the

airway in a death grip. His hands faltered as he struggled for air and the machete touched skin. The burn of fatigue sapped the strength from his muscles.

The African spoke in guttural tones, his voice laced with animal hatred, "I'm going to chop off your hands, you little bastard. Then I'm going to carve out your heart and eat it."

Darkness clouded Bishop's brain. He faintly registered the sickening crunch of a rifle's buttstock connecting with the side of his assailant's head. The pressure on his throat released and the machete-wielding hand was ripped away. He struggled to his feet, gasping to clear his head and regain full consciousness.

"Sir, are you OK?" Mirza asked.

Bishop couldn't hear anything; his mind had blocked out everything but the task at hand. He staggered to recover his pistol from the mud and turned to face the big African who sat dazed on his knees. Blood trickled from the man's mouth and side of his head.

Picking up the machete, he felt the weight in his hand. He inspected the pocked edge of the blade and images of severed arms flashed in his mind. Raising his pistol, he aimed at the man's forehead.

The RUF commander managed a sickly smile. "You're too fucking weak to kill with steel, like a real man."

Bishop holstered the Browning. Rage fueled his muscles. He raised the machete high with both hands and drove it down, his body almost pitching forward with the force. The blade smashed through the man's forehead, cleaving it apart like a block of wood under an axe. Blood and brain matter sprayed up Bishop's arms. The man's eyes rolled back, one either side of the rusted blade wedged in his face.

He released his grip, and with a guttural moan the dead body fell backward, the machete protruding from his head, limp arms splayed out on the ground. For a few seconds he watched the corpse spasm before shock hit him hard like a punch to the gut. Fuck! That could have been me, he thought.

Mirza grasped his arm, dragging him to his senses. The Indian lectured, "Sir, you can't always rely on yourself. A single straw is useless, but together, many straws make a broom."

What? Broom? His thoughts muddled, Bishop rubbed at his throat, leaning wearily on the corporal. "Is that the same straw that broke the camel's back, Mirza?" he croaked. "What are you, a fucking philosopher now?" His words sounded ungrateful but the expression on his face told a different story. "Thanks, mate."

"You're more than welcome, sir. You will be happy to know we have secured the camp," Mirza said, "and I have moved the vehicles down."

"Did you get the rest of those bastards?"

"We killed ten of them; any others must have fled. We won't see them again, at least for today."

Bishop nodded and with the aid of Mirza's shoulder, staggered back to the center of the camp.

The remainder of the UN peacekeepers had already moved up to assist the traumatized refugees as they tended to their injured and dead. The convoy was now parked in the camp's central square and the soldiers were distributing what limited supplies they had.

Wails of grief rent the air as relatives filtered back from the jungle and located family members: dead, maimed, or unconscious. Bishop surveyed the scattered bodies, slain gunmen lying among the slaughtered refugees.

Propping himself up against a sheet of sun-warmed, corrugated iron, he stared blankly at the armless body of the boy. One of the Indians was attempting to find the child's pulse. The soldier shook his head; it was futile. The ground around the boy's body was soaked with blood. The Indian's combat trousers stained crimson at the knees where he knelt by the boy.

Bishop stared at his trembling hands; they too were covered in blood. Tears welled in his eyes as thoughts of blame assaulted him. Did his indecisiveness cost that child his life? Could he have saved the boy with one well-aimed shot? He noticed some of the refugees watching him and forced his head to clear. Struggling to his feet, he stumbled to the medic, who was working intently on a young girl.

"Is there anything I can do?"

The medic looked up, face gaunt and pale. "Yes, thank you, sir. This one needs a splint."

"Is it just her arm?"

"Yes, sir, her arm is badly broken and she is going into shock."

"OK, I'll help this one. You take care of the others." Bishop knelt next to the girl. Forgetting his own fatigue, he carefully tucked a reflective space blanket around the tiny body.

As the young officer worked on splinting the arm, Colonel Kapur strolled over and watched. Growing impatient, the senior officer tapped Bishop on the shoulder.

"Lieutenant! I've contacted UN HQ and we have been ordered to return to base immediately. You need to explain yourself to the force commander!"

Bishop's fists clenched and he stood slowly. Anger flared, then subsided as he looked down at the frail body wrapped in the silver space blanket.

"If you don't mind, sir, I would like to make sure we provide all the assistance we can," he said wearily.

The colonel nodded, content that at least a portion of authority was back in his hands. He was happy to entertain Bishop's philanthropic ways in exchange for a little civility. When they returned to Freetown, the trigger-happy lieutenant would be put in his place.

Grab your copy...
vinci-books.com/primal-unleashed

About the Author

Jack Silkstone grew up on a steady diet of Tom Clancy, James Bond, Jason Bourne, Commando comics, and the original first-person shooters, Wolfenstein and Doom. His background includes a career in military intelligence and special operations, working alongside some of the world's most elite units. His love of action-adventure stories, his military background, and his real-world experiences combined to inspire the no-holds-barred PRIMAL series.